Jetsetters

By
S J Crabb

Copyrighted Material

Copyright © S J Crabb 2017

S J Crabb has asserted her rights under the Copyright, Designs and Patents Act 1988 to be identified as the Author of this work.

This book is a work of fiction and except in the case of historical fact, any resemblance to actual persons, living or dead, is purely coincidental.
All rights reserved. No part of this book may be reproduced or transmitted in any form without written permission of the author, except by a reviewer who may quote brief passages for review purposes only

Also by S J Crabb

<u>Romantic Comedy:</u>
The Diary of Madison Brown
My Perfect Life at Cornish Cottage
My Christmas Boyfriend

<u>Romantic Suspense</u>
The Hardcastle Saga
#1 The One That Got Away
#2 A Matter of Trust
#3 Payback

<u>Paranormal Romance</u>
The Devil's Children
Scarlett
Falcondell
Falcondell Part Two
Lucas
Savannah
Marius
Ashley
Caleb

Check them out at:

<u>sjcrabb.com</u>

Note from The Author

In all my Chick Lit books, there is a little bit of me. Some of the situations come straight from personal experience. Not all of it my story but something I have known happen.

One review on Amazon said that The Diary of Madison Brown was full of unrealistic events.

I would say that life is full of unrealistic events that happen to ordinary people. When you read Jetsetters, I will let you wonder which things are based on true events and which ones are just figments of my very wild imagination. Like I said - there is a lot of me in these books and for those of you who know me, nothing will surprise you.

Now fasten your seat belts, you're in for a turbulent ride.

Dedication

This book is dedicated to my beloved Monarch Airlines who sadly closed for business this year. I worked for Monarch from the age of 19 for five glorious years. I made many friends, some of who I still see today.

It was a fabulous life and the majority of events that happen in this story are based on true experiences – Not all of them I hasten to say!

So, this story is dedicated to Monarch Airlines and all who flew with this great company. In particular my friend Jo who was with them until the bitter end. The end of an era but not forgotten.

(Please note, Jo the character in this story is not meant to depict my friend Jo. I just wanted to name her after such a fantastic stewardess and friend.)

I hope you enjoy seeing what your crew get up to on a stopover! You will never look at them in the same way again.

Chapter 1

"Now breathe! Deep breaths, in-out-in-out."

"Oh, this is absurd. How many more times is she going to do this."

Throwing my friend, for want of a better word, my best Anne Robinson scowl, I turn back to the extremely nervous one gulping for air in front of me.

"It's ok, Jenny. There's nothing to worry about. You do know it's the safest form of travel, don't you?"

She takes a deep breath and looks at me with gratitude swimming in her baby blue eyes.

"Thanks, Becca. I'm so sorry, I don't know why I let it get to me."

I smile and give her a hug as Rachel looks at us with a worried expression.

"Do you think she'll be ok? I mean, it's a long flight. What if she really freaks out and tries to open the door? I've heard these things happen all the time."

Jo rolls her eyes and huffs.

"For goodness' sake, all of you. Pull yourself together, Jenny, this is getting way out of hand. You're stronger than this and I'm beginning to feel a panic attack of my own coming on at the thought of a week with you lot. I mean, it's not as if my life isn't in chaos at the moment and this is all I need."

Sighing heavily, I smile at Jenny reassuringly.

"Take as long as you need. There's no point in working yourself up. We've got plenty of time before take-off. Maybe you should just sit quietly for a minute and gather yourself together."

Jo snorts beside me.

"Oh yes, take all the time you need. After all, it's not as if the passengers aren't going to arrive any minute. The sight of their fearless crew is really going to instil confidence in them. For god's sake, Jenny, pull yourself together and remember your training."

My heart sinks as Jenny's eyes fill up again and I glare over at Jo. She just raises her eyes.

"What? I tell it how it is. There's no point in pandering to her. This has been getting worse ever since her mum died and she needs to snap out of it."

"Jo!"

She shrugs.

"Just saying. Anyway, Rachel swap with Jenny and we'll keep her out of sight in the galley. You'll have to take her position. This is all I need, a crew member afraid of flying and no Captain. This is not getting off to a good start."

Jenny looks at her with a stricken expression and my patience starts to wear thin. Taking her hand, I smile softly.

"Come on, Jenny, lets' go and make ourselves busy. It will take your mind off it. We'll leave Jo to go and boss the rest of them around. You'll be fine, trust me."

Jenny sniffs and smiles gratefully as Jo looks at us angrily.

"This is all I need. One Captain down and four hundred passengers about to descend on us; they are probably drunk already and singing, 'Loco in Acapulco' at the top of their voices. To cap it all, Jenny is having a meltdown and I'm in my own private emotional hell."

I smile, but any sympathy I have for her is fading fast. I know Jo is having major problems, but the priority is Jenny. She has just lost her mum, and it's hit her hard. She never moved out, and it was just the two of them for most of her life. She was always timid and insecure and now she is hanging by a thread. The fear of flying started after the funeral. She was always a nervous person but never this bad. Now she fears her own shadow.

This trip was meant to bring her out of herself and bring some light to her now dark life. It's not starting well.

Then it gets a whole lot worse as Jo hisses angrily.

"Oh, for god's sake this can't be happening. What the hell is he doing here?"

We look up and my heart sinks as I see the Captain entering the cabin sheepishly. Great, it just gets better and better.

He smiles at us nervously and disappears quickly into the cockpit where his First Officer is carrying out the pre-flight checks. Jo looks at us with a look of pure and deadly, murderous intent.

"Well, if he thinks I'm going anywhere with him, then he's got another thing coming. He's done this on purpose, you mark my words."

I reach out and pull her back before she marches in there and lets rip.

"Calm down, Jo. It will be fine. I expect he was all they had."

Jo glares at me but I note the mist in her eyes. I feel bad for her. Pete is—was, her boyfriend. They have just had a major bust up and was another reason to come on this trip. She needed to get away and so we engineered this trip for the four of us. One week's stopover in Acapulco. Fun city, full of tequila shots and endless days sunbathing. Just what we all need—to leave our inhibitions behind and let ourselves go for once. It's not often we all get rostered on a trip together and this took some engineering. If Pete is joining us, then it's going to be one hell of a bumpy ride.

Rachel sighs heavily.

"This just gets better and better. Now, all we need is a bunch of unruly passengers, a medical emergency and to run out of gin on the first drinks run. If anyone wants me, I'll be drowning my sorrows in First Class."

She walks away and Jenny stares after her sadly.

"I'm sorry, guys. I'll try to pull myself together. Becca's right, I just need to keep busy to take my mind off it."

"Ladies, ladies, stop your gossiping and let's rock-and-roll. I just spoke to dreamy, sex on legs, handling guy and he told me the wheelchairs are on their way."

We look up and see Marcus, one of the Stewards, heading towards us. Jo looks at me and shakes her head.

"Whatever, I don't have time for this. Come on everyone, get to your positions, we've got a flight to operate."

As we head towards our positions my heart sinks, as Jo smiles in a slightly maniacal, mass murderer, serial killer kind of way and says darkly, "He's going to wish he never came."

~*~*~*~*~

Chapter 2

"Ooh, he's nice."

Marcus nods and smiles flirtatiously at a rather handsome man heading down the tunnel towards us. Fighting back a grin, I smile at him politely and take a look at his boarding pass.

"Turn right, halfway down the second cabin on your right."

He smiles and heads off as Marcus checks out his behind and whispers.

"I'd join the mile-high club with him."

I snort. "I thought you joined that years ago."

His eyes twinkle and he shrugs.

"What can I say, I like to keep my *member-ship* up."

I snort, quickly turning it into a cough as a family descends on us with confusion all over their faces. They look around them in awe as we direct them to their seats.

Only three hundred more to go.

It's at times like this I envy Rachel living it up in First Class. She gets the easy ride, while I serve up drinks, meal, and duty-free to the masses. At least I have Marcus to keep me entertained. The time should pass quickly enough.

I have worked at Jet Air for ten years now. Far from being just a job, it's now a way of life. I couldn't imagine doing anything else, despite how much I moan about it. The trouble is, if I didn't have this I would have nothing. I live alone in a flat near the airport. My family lives in Milton Keynes and I rarely see them. All of my friends live nearby and yet our timetables dictate that we are rarely off at the same time. Over the years it has become increasingly hard to meet anyone worth holding onto and I've become a bit of a cat lady—minus the cat. Just me and my potted plant

Malcolm to care for and I have never felt so lonely. I thought I'd be married with kids by now. Not even close. The only men I meet are on Tinder and after the last one I'm seriously thinking of deleting my profile. How did it all go so wrong?

Marcus nudges me.

"Hottie alert - incoming. Cue the romantic love music."

As I look up, my heart flutters and everything else tunes out. Wow! My fantasy male is heading purposefully towards us and now I can't think of anything else but how much I want him to be mine. Immediately, my mind wanders as I live out our life together in two seconds flat. We are married and in love. Our family consists of two adorable children - one of each, possibly called Kitty and Oscar. We live in a pretty house with roses around the door and drive a Range Rover. Ours is the perfect life and we want for nothing.

"Let me show you to your seat, Sir. I'm going that way, so it will be no trouble."

What!? I beam back to earth just in time to see Marcus leading my new husband towards the front of the cabin.

"Excuse me, Miss, but we have been separated and I have a child under five who can't be expected to travel with strangers. The girl at the check-in desk told me to ask when we got on board."

I shake myself and focus on the job at hand. My heart melts as I look at the sweet little boy holding onto his mother's hand with terrified eyes. His mother is looking at me anxiously and the father looks as if he will kill me on the spot if I don't do as he asks.

I smile reassuringly.

"No problem. If you would just wait to the side, I will see what I can do."

I head off to find Jo. She oversees the flight and will sort them out, I have no doubt in my mind. Nobody messes with her and it may take her mind off twenty ways to get revenge without going to prison.

By the time I offload the problem and resume my position, Marcus is back looking extremely smug.

Quickly, I whisper, "Well?"

He smirks and his eyes blaze with excitement.

"Oh my god, Becca. I haven't been so excited since Dario Brady dressed as the biker from The Village People for Gay pride. I almost want to scream like a young girl at a One Direction concert. He is sooo hot."

I nod vigorously.

"Yes, I know that. What did you find out? Is he travelling alone? Was there a ring on his finger? Is he gay? Come on, tell me everything."

Marcus smirks again.

"Well. He's sitting in 12A and so far, the seat next to him is empty. He didn't say much, but he had that Alpha Male, brooding dominant look to him that I love."

Marcus starts fanning himself with the safety card and looks around him conspiratorially.

"I'll find out everything I can by the time we get to Mexico. If there's even a small chance he's available, then I will be on him like a sombrero on a donkey at the seaside."

Laughing to myself, I carry on greeting the passengers. Suddenly, this flight has got a lot more interesting.

Once the passengers are on board, we start securing the cabin. I can't stop checking out 12A whenever possible and must admit he's absolutely gorgeous. His hair is slightly long on top with blonde tips. His body looks like the sort that grace most Kindle covers these days and his white t-shirt is straining against the muscles underneath. His arms are inked, and he is wearing beige combat trousers and trainers. I stifle a sigh every time I look at him and wonder what his story is.

The seat next to him remains empty—thankfully and I dream about sitting next to him on our way to our honeymoon.

"Excuse me, Miss, but do you have anything for motion sickness?"

My desire filled thoughts are interrupted by a woman in row 14. I smile and head off to the galley to fetch the pills.

Just before the plane reaches the end of the runway we take to our jump seats and Marcus whispers, "So far so good with 12A. He's alone, and that means fair game. I'll suss him out and report back."

I look at him feeling annoyed.

"Why you? I could suss him out as well. Why do you get to monopolise him?"

Marcus winks.

"Because that's my section and I'm a professional. If he sat in F-J, then he would be yours. Sorry, it's the rules."

He grins as I glower at him.

"Ok, but remember he's mine if he's straight."

We bump fists.

"Deal!"

~*~*~*~*~

Chapter 3

Almost as soon as the seatbelt sign goes off the phone rings in the galley. My heart sinks as I hear Pete whisper urgently.

"Hey, Becca. Can you come up here, please?"

"Ok, I won't be a second."

I leave Marcus to set up the drinks trolley and head to the flight deck. Luckily, Jo is pre-occupied at the rear of the aircraft, so I head inside.

Barry Jolly, the First Officer, turns and smiles.

"Hi, Becca. Are you looking forward to some fun in the sun?"

I nod, smiling. I like Barry. He's great fun and has been on a few of my trips before.

Pete looks at me anxiously.

"Listen, you know how this works. Jo is out for me and this is a long flight. Make sure you prepare everything that comes in here and don't leave anything to her. I've lived with her long enough to know the tricks you girls pull and I don't trust her an inch."

I giggle and roll my eyes.

"I'll try, but you know how determined she is."

Barry looks intrigued.

"What happened?"

Pete pulls a face.

"She's overreacting as usual. Apparently, I called her by another name when we were in the middle of it one night. I don't know why, I don't even know a Margaret. Well, you can imagine what happened next and now she thinks I'm having an affair with Margaret, whoever she is."

We burst out laughing as he shakes his head.

"I know, it's bad, isn't it? The trouble is, no matter what I say she doesn't believe me. She's intent on finding out who Margaret is and won't let me near her."

Barry's shoulders start shaking and I cling to the back of the seat for support. It's actually really funny but must have been devastating for Jo. She is crazy stupid in love with Pete - sorry was and sees this as the ultimate betrayal.

I try to get a grip and smile sympathetically.

"I'll try, leave it with me. You do know you will have a rough trip though."

He shakes his head miserably.

"I know. As soon as they called me out when Dennis went sick I knew it would be a bad move. I'm just hoping that I get the chance to convince her it was all a mistake."

I smile but he sees the doubt in my eyes and sighs.

"Anyway, I just thought I'd protect myself as much as possible before she gets started."

I leave them to it and head back to the galley. Marcus has already got things sorted so I make us a quick cup of tea as well as the ones for the pilots.

Just before I finish, Jo appears looking annoyed.

"You know, Jenny is still a mess back there. This flight is going to be hard work in more ways than one. I've told Caitlyn to keep an eye on her and let me know if she crumbles."

She spies the drinks and a wicked spark ignites in her eyes.

"Is that for Pete?"

I nod, and she smiles wickedly.

"I'll take it in."

Shaking my head, I look at her nervously.

"Do you think that's such a good idea?"

She shrugs.

"I'm a professional, Becca. Just because he turned out to be some sort of cheating playboy, it doesn't mean I'm about to compromise my professional standards."

She grabs the drinks and smiles wickedly.

"He won't know that though. As far as he knows, I will have put something rank in his drink and my bet is he won't drink a drop. It's all psychological you know. Sometimes, doing nothing reaps the greatest rewards."

Marcus raises his eyes and throws me 'the look' as she heads off to the flight deck.

"She's right you know. He will be a nervous wreck by the time we land, and she won't have done a thing. It's the power of the mind."

A call bell goes off and we eagerly look to see if we need to fight to the death to get to 12A. No such luck and I get lumbered while Marcus carries on filling the ice bucket.

I make sure that I wiggle through the cabin with my best runway walk past 12A. I am slightly disappointed to note that he is looking out of the window.

Once I have helped a lady retrieve her bag from the overhead compartment, I walk slowly back.

This time he has his headphones on and his eyes shut. Short of pretending there is turbulence and falling across his lap I just head back to work.

As I walk, I wonder why I have been affected by him so much. I've done this job for ten years and seen many a hot guy on board. I have never reacted with this desperation before. I blame that date from Tinder. It obviously sent me over the edge and flagged up that I am back to square one again. After being cooped up with a brick collecting maniac for four hours, it's surprising that I haven't rushed out and joined a convent.

Who collects bricks? Ever! I sat through four tedious hours of feigning interest while Rufus told me every type out there and how they are made. I could tell you the differences in their manufacture and their histories and list their selling points. I wouldn't mind, but he said he was into building a future with someone and enjoyed walks in the country and West End shows. The last time I checked, Bob the Builder wasn't playing. Well, that's a part of my life I'll never get back.

I try to push all thoughts of men from my mind as I start the drinks service. Mostly the passengers are nice, and I enjoy my job. I try not to glance over at row 12 but can't resist when I draw near. I see Marcus hand him a can of coke and a packet of pretzels. I stifle a grin as I see Marcus in full charm mode. If 12A is gay, he won't stand a chance. I feel happy to note that he just smiles and turns back to the screen he is watching. Marcus catches my eye and winks as we move on.

Once the drinks trolleys are stowed away, we start to organise the meals. As we work Jo appears with a bottle of champagne.

"Here you go, Becca. This one's for a passenger in your section. Marcus, I need you to heat up Pete and Barry's meals and make sure I get to take them in."

Marcus grins and I roll my eyes. Whatever!

I look down at the envelope and do a double take. Whoa, I'm in luck. Marcus is none the wiser, and this champagne is for 12A. This is it. The moment my life will change forever. He will look up and our eyes will meet. He will hold my gaze and the world will stand still. We will bow to the pull of the inevitable and he will immediately declare his undying love for me. This is it - I can feel it.

With a deep breath, I walk towards him, my heart pounding and my knees buckling. I ignore an outstretched arm willing me to stop and have only one focus in mind. 12A!

I pretend to look around as if locating the seat. I glance down at the envelope and then check the numbers above the seats.

Then I gaze at him and flash him my sexiest smile.

"Excuse me, Sir. You have been sent a bottle of complimentary champagne."

He looks up in surprise and his gaze falls to the bottle. I see a look of resignation enter his eyes as he sighs and smiles thinly.

"Thank you."

Taking the printed sheet from the envelope, I start to read the message.

"There's a message I need to read out, apparently."

He looks at me with interest and his eyes twinkle and a slow smile breaks out. God, that smile is captivating. I have almost forgotten there is anyone else on board. I realise I am staring and cough nervously.

"Right then, here it is."
I take a deep breath.

"Congratulations on your wedding my old mucker. Take a gulp of this to get you in the mood to..."

Suddenly, I'm aware of the shocked faces around me. The lady behind looks at me with shock as her husband snorts and looks away. There is silence and I feel the blush creeping up from my toes to my cheeks. 12A looks amused and grins, a mouth-watering, panty melting grin that almost makes me pass out.

"Thanks, I think I'll take that."

He reaches out and as I hand him the note his fingers brush against mine. Fighting the urge to grab them and never let go, I try to compose myself.

"Um, well, good. Yes, that's good, um very good."

To my extreme horror, I am now rambling incoherently, and his amused stare isn't helping. Shaking myself, I try to snap out of it and smile professionally.

"Would you like me to open it?"

Trying not to think of opening anything else for him, I look at him coolly.

He shakes his head.

"Not on my account, but you could offer it around to my neighbours here."

The shock appears to have dissolved around me at his words and the woman behind giggles.

"Oh, super. We love champagne, don't we, Rory? That's very kind of you."

The others murmur their thanks and I smile.

"Ok then, drinks all round."

I head off and think about what just happened. He's just got married. Of course, he has, why would I think he would be single? In fact, he should have been married off years ago. Guys like him don't stay unattached for long.

Big disappointment crashing down and my world has now ended. Dreams dashed and hopes unfulfilled—again!

Marcus is as upset as I am when I tell him what happened.

"Do you think it was a gay marriage?" he asks hopefully. I shake my head.

"No, I think the note was designed to rhyme with her. It would explain the vacant seat beside him. Where do you think she is? She must have missed the flight or something. Maybe they are going to Mexico to get married and she will join him later."

Marcus looks thoughtful.

"I expect he 'came out' when faced with declaring his love before God. It weighed too heavily on his mind and he couldn't go on living a lie. I expect he's going to Mexico to discover himself and bag a hot new boyfriend. Oh well, it's a win-win for me if it is."

Despite my devastation, I laugh.

"Keep on telling yourself that, Marcus."

He shrugs.

"Oh well. I'm over him already. The guy in 16C keeps on giving me the signals, so I'll transfer my attention to him instead."

He sets off with his meal cart and I envy his ability to switch feelings so quickly. However, I'm devastated, and I don't know why.

~*~*~*~

Chapter 4

Throughout the meal service, I keep on thinking of 12A. I wonder what it must be like to marry somebody like that. His wife must be some sort of supermodel and totally gorgeous. I'm not even sure how I reach the end of the service because I don't remember a thing.

By the time I head out to serve the coffee my mind is obsessed. I try not to let him affect me, but as I walk towards him with my coffee pot, I feel the butterflies in my stomach and my heart hammering.

I smile, with what I think is a professional, cool, detached smile and say brightly,

"Coffee, Sir?"

He looks up and I almost drop the pot. The smile he flashes me is one hundred percent sex god.

"Thanks."

His voice is deep and sexy, and his accent is more public school than I would have thought. He may have a certain rough charm, but his accent is smooth and privileged. Could he get any better?

My hand shakes as I pour the coffee and I try to take deep breaths. What is the matter with me?

It must take all of two seconds, but this exchange will keep me company in my private thoughts for the whole trip. This is my moment with my dream man and I will replay every wink of the eye, every smile and every gesture on repeat for the rest of my trip.

Then I move on and leave my head in the seat next to him.

Back in the galley I try to compose myself and pretend he isn't here. I am becoming some sort of stalker obsessed mad woman after just one look from a stranger.

Deciding a change of scenery is in order, I head off to visit Rachel in First Class.

She sees me coming and smiles happily.

"Hey, how are things back there?"

I shake my head and roll my eyes.

"Well, a bit hot actually. There appears to be my fantasy male sitting in 12A who had grabbed my attention and I can't focus on anything but him. The trouble is, he is on his honeymoon or on the way to his wedding. Life sucks."

She grins and raises her eyes.

"You need a man, honey - desperately."

I nod miserably.

"It would appear that I do. I am obsessing over a stranger and can't think straight."

She leans forward and whispers.

"There's a super-hot guy in row 1. He appears to be on his own and seems cute. Why don't you go and check him out? Take him this drink, I was just heading that way."

I smile thankfully. Great, some distraction therapy - just what the doctor ordered.

I head to the front of the aircraft and note the difference in this cabin. Everything is calmer and more organised than the obvious chaos behind it. People are stretched out on their reclining bed seats and watching films, or playing on their iPads.

I reach row 1 and look at the guy working away on his computer. He seems nice, not in the panty-melting, sex god man of my dreams way of 12A. No, more like your professional businessman on a trip. The type to take you to dinner and buy you flowers, before providing you with 2.5

children and a nice house in the suburbs. After 12A he seems boring.

Sighing inwardly, I smile and offer him the drink.

"Your drink, sir."

I note the surprise in his eyes as he reaches out to take the glass from my tray.

"Oh, thank you. I haven't seen you before; where have you been hiding?"

I laugh, feeling a little awkward.

"In another section. I'm just helping out here for a while."

He leans back and looks at me as though he is ripping the clothes off my body. Far from being hot, it just feels creepy. He licks his lips and interest sparks in his eyes.

"So, tell me. How long is your stopover in Acapulco?"

My heart starts beating a little faster. Wow, he doesn't hold back. I can see the meaning behind those words and just smile sweetly.

"We have a week, luckily. Are you on business or pleasure?"

Pleasure! Why use that word. He is now almost panting.

"Business, but I am up for a bit of pleasure if it comes my way. Where are you staying, maybe we could meet up for a drink one evening?"

Oh no, trust me to start a conversation with Mr sleaze. Just the way he is raking me with his eyes is making me feel cheap.

I shake my head and smile coldly.

"I doubt that. We have very strict rules on staying with the crew. I won't be allowed to mingle with the passengers. It's against company policy. Anyway, enjoy your trip."

I turn to go, and he calls me back.

"Here, take my card. Even if we can't meet up in Acapulco, maybe we could continue this conversation back at home. I promise you I'm not some weirdo. I just happen to enjoy meeting gorgeous women who spark my interest. Call me if you want a night out."

Taking his card, I smile politely.

"Thanks. Anyway, I had better get back."

I feel his eyes burning a hole in my back as I make my way back to Rachel. She sees the card in my hand and looks excited.

"Wow, that was fast work. I told you he seemed nice."

I shudder and pull a face.

"Nice isn't the word I'd use. He was really creepy as it happened. A fast worker who made his intentions clear after just one look. Not my type at all."

She looks thoughtful.

"He may be ok for some hot sex though."

Pushing her, I make the cringe face.

"Yuk, wash that thought from your mind. He was totally creepy and definitely not my type. I'm heading back to the normality of the masses and leave your rampant businessmen to you."

As I head back, I realise that I still have the card in my hand. Maybe she does have a point. He may be my only option and is fifty times better than brick man. I could use him for sex and move on. Ok, now I feel sick. That's not me despite how much I wish it was. It's exactly why I am still single after all these years. I want the perfect man and the dream life. I don't settle for second best and it's got me absolutely nowhere.

~*~*~*~*~

Chapter 5

Marcus grins as I head back to the galley. Pulling a face, I rip the card in two and throw it in the gash bin.

"Don't ask! Some creepy guy in First Class just propositioned me with the promise of a wild night in Mexico. It would probably end up with me beneath him or against some wall in a dark alley."

I see Marcus smirk as I hear a cough behind me. Spinning around, I see 12A leaning against the galley wall with amusement in his eyes. I feel the heat rising and just stare at him in horror. Did he just hear that? From the expression on his face he did and now he must think I'm some sort of cheap hussy.

I stutter.

"Um… can I get you anything? I mean, a drink or something, you know, like a drink."

Marcus grins and I feel the embarrassment consume me. Why does this man reduce me to a gibbering wreck?

He smiles, and my heart beats a little faster.

"Sorry, I just wondered if I could grab a glass of water."

In a rather high voice, I squeak. "Of course."

I turn to grab a glass and Marcus says quickly.

"I believe congratulations are in order."

I freeze and wait for his answer as if it's the answer to world peace. I think I must be holding my breath because time stands still.

He says in a soft voice.

"Thanks. The trouble is I appear to be on my honeymoon without a bride."

Marcus looks interested.

"Where is she then?"

12A laughs softly.

"I'm not sure. Probably still explaining to my brother why she jilted him at the altar."

I almost drop the glass I'm filling with water as Marcus gasps.

"Wow, this is one story I must hear. Carry on and leave nothing out. I want to hear every detail."

He shakes his head.

"It's a long story. The result is I am now on their honeymoon all alone and just looking forward to the fact that I am well away from the storm back in England. It was a tough call, but somebody had to volunteer, otherwise it would be a waste."

I hand him the glass and my hand shakes as he smiles at me.

"Thanks."

He doesn't move and just takes a sip and I swear my heart pants as I watch his lips wrap around the glass. I am now officially out of control.

Suddenly, we hear, "This way, please. Now, remember, the password is Margaret."

What?!

I see Jo leading a woman towards the flight deck and she winks as she passes. The woman is giggling and says, "Oh. My. God. I can't believe I'm going in. I've always wanted to see inside a cockpit. It's my ultimate fantasy."

We all look in disbelief as Jo leads the woman inside. When she comes out, I pounce on her.

"What's going on?"

She grins wickedly.

"If he wants a Margaret, then I have approximately one hundred ready to go. I'm telling them that only people named Margaret are allowed in today, so they must answer to that. By the time he gets to Mexico he will hate the sound of that name. Every person I send in will be his worst nightmare."

She scans the rows behind us and settles on the elderly woman in 18B. "Perfect, she will be my next visitor."

Marcus laughs and 12A looks bemused. Shaking my head, I say wearily, "Don't ask."

We turn our attention back to 12A and Marcus says with interest.

"Why did she jilt him - do you know?"

He shakes his head.

"I heard she had second thoughts. Apparently, she saw a medium the week before who told her she would marry a fighter pilot called Tony. My brother is a painter and decorator called Gary. It messed with her brain and planted doubt in her mind She thought she was making a terrible mistake and needed to be available for Tony when he showed up."

We all look at each other in disbelief and then burst out laughing. Marcus wipes his eyes as we hear a call bell.

"I'll go. Wait there, handsome, I haven't finished with you yet. I want all the gory details on my return."

Then we are alone - well, as alone as we can be on a metal tube with four hundred other people within touching distance.

Suddenly, I feel awkward. The galley is small, and he is large in more than just his size. He fills my mind as well as my personal space and I smile nervously.

"So, can I get you anything else?"

He smiles, and I almost sigh out loud.

"A coke would be good."

Thankful for something to take my mind off the desire to leap on him and cling on for dear life, I set about getting the coke.

He laughs softly. "So, I suppose it's an occupational hazard to get hit on by your passengers."

I almost drop the coke and feel myself blushing. He did hear! I just shrug and roll my eyes.

"Not really. It doesn't happen that often - luckily. I mean, if you saw the guy you would agree I had a lucky escape. I think some people think we come with the price of the ticket."

He looks at me thoughtfully and if I could I would stamp on my own foot. What an idiot. If that didn't say 'stay away' I don't know what would.

The silence is a bit awkward, so I grab the glass, fill it with ice and open the can. What the…? Coke bursts forth like the fountain at Trafalgar square and lands all over his pristine white t-shirt. I don't know who is more shocked, me or him, as I watch the coke dripping from his hair and running down his neck.

Grabbing the tea towel, I start attacking him mercilessly saying with total horror,

"Oh my god, I'm so sorry. It's the pressure you know. It does that sometimes. Please let me help you."

He raises his eyes to mine and smiles.

"It's fine. I'll just take it off and rinse it in the sink if I may?"

Swallowing hard, I nod and holy mother of all things sexy, he takes off his t-shirt right in front of me and I absolutely stare at him shamelessly.

His body is every inch what I expected, and I think I must be drooling because quite frankly I must have died and gone to heaven. Wow and double wow. This guy should work for the dream boys. Actually - maybe he does. Come to think of it he could be anything.

He raises his eyes and smirks as he catches me gawping at him like a teenager. I feel decidedly hot and just grab his t-shirt and babble incoherently.

"Don't worry... um... yes... this is good... water... I need water... yes or soda, maybe that would work."

Suddenly, we hear, "Good god, Becca. You didn't waste any time. I've only been gone two minutes you brazen hussy."

Marcus stands there looking like all his prayers have been answered as he openly stares at 12A's chest. Far from looking awkward 12A just smiles sexily. Ok, he must be a dream boy and used to this sort of attention.

Marcus shakes his head and says with authority.

"Don't panic, I always carry a spare t-shirt in my crew bag. I keep it with my paper knickers - always on hand for any emergency. You can wear that, and I'll try to get yours washed and dry before we land."

He heads to the overhead locker and I mouth - 'sorry' - to 12A, who just smiles as if he's finding this whole situation very entertaining.

Marcus comes back and thrusts a similar white t-shirt to 12A. "Here, try this on for size."

We watch with total disappointment as he covers his amazing body with the borrowed t-shirt. Then we all laugh when it becomes evident that Marcus is several sizes smaller than the man mountain in front of us. It clings to his bulges and accentuates them further. His arm burst out and I fear that it will rip if he moves.

Marcus grins.

"So, Mr 12A, tell me your name so I can stalk you shamelessly until you return my t-shirt."

He laughs softly.

"Sorry, I'm Luke."

Marcus grins. "I'm Marcus and this is Becca. So where are you staying in Mexico? We could all meet up if you're on your own."

I find that I'm holding my breath waiting for his answer.

"The Emporio."

Marcus looks at me and we can't stop the grin from spreading across our faces.

"Snap. Who'd have thought."

The curtain twitches and Jo pushes her way into the now extremely crowded galley.

"Oh, sorry. Listen, Becca, I don't suppose you could check on Jenny for me? I'm flat out with Margarets and haven't got time. You know, this trip could end up much more fun than I thought. I've thought of loads of ways to get my revenge and this is just the beginning."

Smiling apologetically at Luke, I head out to check on Jenny. Jo's words ring in my ears as I go, and I have to agree - this trip is definitely going to be more fun than I thought.

~*~*~*~*~

Chapter 6

Jenny is busy in the rear galley and smiles as I enter.
"Hey, Becca. How are things at your end?"
I laugh happily.
"Couldn't be better. It appears that my prayers have been answered in the form of some serious eye candy for the trip ahead."
She looks intrigued.
"Ok. Spill everything."
"Well, one of our passengers, who has just stripped to the waist in the galley, is staying at our hotel. He is luckily travelling alone and in need of some company. I have left Marcus to iron out all the details because as we know he won't let him get away in a hurry."
Jenny laughs. "I can't wait to meet him. Do you fancy a cuppa? I think things have quietened down a bit."
I nod and pull out the jump seat and sit down.
"So, tell me, how have things been since the funeral?"
She smiles sadly.
"Lonely. It was just me and mum for all of my life and now it's just me. The house feels big and cold and I don't know the first thing about doing anything. My Aunt and Uncle have been amazing, but they won't be around forever. I know I have to try to make a life for myself but it's scaring me."
Reaching out, I grab her hand.
"You're not on your own. I'm in the same position as you, really. I know I still have my parents, but they live so far away. It's just me and Malcolm the potted plant and I agree, life is scary when you're on your own. Maybe we could spend more time together. You could always stay at my flat if you like and we could be lonely together."

Jenny's eyes fill with tears, and she hugs me tightly.

"You're a great friend, Becca."

I swallow the lump in my throat.

"You too, Jenny."

Pulling back, I roll my eyes.

"Look at us, what a pair. You do know we're going to have an amazing trip though. I can just feel it deep down."

She laughs.

"Yes, despite the drama with Jo and Pete, I think it will do us all good to get away."

Caitlyn rushes in.

"The man in 30B wants a gin and tonic. I could so use one myself right now."

I nod in agreement.

"Just make sure we grab as much as we can on landing. Who's having the crew room this time?"

Caitlyn shrugs.

"Maybe Marcus, I'm not sure."

Jenny laughs.

"Well, it sure as eggs won't be you, Becca."

I look at her in horror.

"You're right there. I couldn't think of anything worse. I'd be on edge the whole time."

Caitlyn looks interested as Jenny grins.

"Our Becca is a serious OCD freak. She hates anything out of place and carries wet wipes in her handbag. The thought of one can out of place or a packet of unopened crisps on the floor would send her into a complete meltdown."

I laugh at Caitlyn's expression.

"It's a good job I live alone. Jenny's right, I hate anything out of place. It's ok at work because it's not my own space but at home - I'm a nightmare."

After spending a pleasant tea break with the girls, I head off back to work and the Duty-Free service.

Once the service is over, I get another call from the flight deck.

"Becca, tell Jo no more Margaret's. If one more comes through this door, I'm going to spin this bird in a loop the loop and make you sit with your seatbelts on for the rest of the flight. Oh, and a cup of untampered with tea would be nice with some crew biscuits."

I laugh to myself. Somebody is decidedly feeling the strain and I feel sorry for him.

As soon as the coast is clear, I take him the tea and usher the latest Margaret out. I hear the door click behind me and know that he has locked it.

Jo hurries up with another Margaret in tow.

"You didn't let him lock it? Oh great, now I'll have to think of something else."

She hurries off mumbling to herself, while I show the Margaret back to her seat.

Soon the passengers start to fall asleep and we get the chance to eat. This part always drags the most and we are at our most stupid thinking of ways to pass the time and keep the boredom away.

I brave a visit to Rachel and we sit in a couple of spare seats at the back of the cabin and chat about life in general.

Rachel is the only one of us who is married. Her husband, Lorenzo is Italian and works as a chef. They haven't been married long but make a really sweet couple.

She stretches out and shakes off her shoes.

"It's good to sit down and eat something at last."

I nod in agreement.

"You're right there. So, tell me, how is that gorgeous husband of yours?"

She smiles softly.

"He's fine. Keeping busy with the restaurant and I'm busy here so sometimes we are like two ships that pass in the night."

I detect an edge to her voice and wonder if there is something going on. I don't ask though because she is a very private person and isn't one to bare her soul. She will tell us if she wants to but I decide to keep an eye on her. Something is definitely off.

I tell her all about Luke and she looks excited.

"Wow, I can't wait to meet him. You deserve some luck in your life, Becca. You've been alone too long."

I look at her in amazement.

"What, you think he's going to be interested in me? You wait until you see him, Rachel. He could have his pick of the bunch."

She looks at me sternly.

"Then he would pick the best one with you. Don't sell yourself short. You're gorgeous and he would be very lucky to get you."

I think about Luke. Maybe this is fate dealing me a favourable hand. Could it really be too good to be true?

I actually can't wait to find out.

~*~*~*~*~

Chapter 7

By the time we land my excitement is at fever pitch. I have shared many a secret look with Luke and imagined us in every possible situation through life. By the time we land we have dated, married, had babies and live in a gorgeous cottage in Cornwall. He adores me and gave me a sweet little puppy for our twentieth anniversary. His family loves me and we are inseparable and have taken up glamping.

As we wait for the passengers to disembark, I feel worried that this may be the last time I see him. What if we have switched hotels and are staying somewhere else? It would be a disaster.

As he heads our way, I think I'm about to have an anxiety attack. He smiles as he reaches us and Marcus grins.

"Until later, Luke. You can keep the t-shirt if you like. If you do give it back don't worry about washing it."

I cringe at the dirty look Marcus throws his way and Luke laughs.

"Thanks, Marcus. I owe you one."

I snort. "Don't tell him that. You may not like what he wants in return."

Marcus pretends to be annoyed and Luke smiles at me.

"Thank you, Becca. I hope to see you at the Emporio later."

I swear my toes curl up and my heart does a victory dance in my chest. I smile shyly.

"Yes, let's hope so. Have a good journey."

He nods and turns away, leaving me with the uncontrollable urge to run after him and attach myself to his body, forever. Instead, I just sigh and turn my attention back to the job in hand.

After we clear customs and retrieve our luggage, we head off to the hotel. I feel strangely excited and put it down to the fact I may see Luke again. I felt something with him - a sort of chemistry that I can't explain. It sends secret messages to my heart of something that may be about to happen. I hope so because I am running of ideas.

I've tried the online dating thing - absolute nightmare and now I think I'm scarred for life.

I've tried the introductions through friends. This was also a disaster and left me worrying about how well they really know me, given some of the men they have thrown my way. It's almost as if they think - 'Oh, he'll do.' The trouble is, I am very picky and have always wanted the fairy-tale. I have been waiting for that lightning bolt to strike and it hasn't even come close. My mum tells me I should stop being so choosy and what I'm waiting for isn't out there in the real world. Well, she obviously hasn't met Luke. He is everything I think I want. I just hope he doesn't turn out to be a complete dud.

By the time we reach the hotel my mind has planned out the main event in my life, the sequel and then the television series. Becca and Luke, - Luke and Becca - Love at Thirty Thousand Feet- Mile High Love- Steamy Galley. I have written the book and printed the t-shirt and feel like a girl obsessing over a boy in a boy band.

"Look at him - not a care in the world. He doesn't even care that he's broken my heart."

I am brought back to earth as Jo nudges me in the side. I look over and see Pete laughing with Barry as we wait to check in. Jo's eyes narrow.

"He thinks it's a joke but I'm not laughing."

Sighing to myself, I smile sympathetically.

"He may be telling the truth and it was all a misunderstanding."

Jo snorts.

"Misunderstanding! When the love of your life calls you by another woman's name while making love to you, then something is very badly wrong. He was obviously thinking of this Margaret woman and I will find out who she is if it kills me. I've been through the list of everyone at work. The closest I've got is Maggie Parker, but she's married to that doctor and doesn't stop talking about him and their perfect life. I don't think it's her because she isn't really his type. Do you think it could be one of the new intake? Maybe he met her on one of his flights last month. He worked a lot because of the shortage of pilots. I hardly saw him. Come to think of it he did have a night stop in Barcelona. Maybe she was on that trip. I'll ask Sandy in ops when I get back."

The receptionist beckons us over and I am thankful for the distraction. I think Jo is wrong. Pete adores her and I believe his explanation. I wonder why she is finding it so hard to believe him? Maybe that's what love does to you. When you find it, you are so afraid to lose it that it scrambles an otherwise normally rational brain. I hope they work it out because they are so cute together.

The receptionist hands me a form and I fill out my name and contact details. As I pass it back, he hands me one of those room key things and winks.

"Here you go meez. Have a lovely stay at the Emporio. Please, if you need anything come and find me."

He winks again, and I wonder if he has a nervous tick. He holds my gaze and stares at me and smiles and I quickly grab the room key. I know that look. The look of interest that promises more than just a morning wake up call. Well, he can keep his dirty thoughts to himself. Some men see a girl in a uniform and think she is fair game. Well, not this trolly dolly. I have standards that are obviously higher than most men can reach. All except one that is. I wonder where he is?

I leave the others after agreeing to meet in room 217. Marcus got the privilege of the crew room and I think it was a good choice. He is always the last to leave anyway and drinks the most. He also doesn't care about mess or entertaining lots of people in his hotel room. Ugh, I can think of nothing worse.

No, my room must remain orderly at all times with everything in its place just how I like it.

I appear to be the only one left in the lift as everyone else gets out at the floors below mine. I travel to the top floor and feel irritated. Typical, now I will have the furthest to travel down to the pool every day.

It doesn't take me long to reach my room and I notice it is down a little corridor with two rooms facing each other. As I open the door, my mouth drops open and almost hits the plush carpeting inside.

Wow! This room is unbelievable.

I wander in as if in a dreamlike state. The whole of Acapulco bay stretches out before me, the lights bouncing off the sea that it surrounds. Huge sliding doors run the width of the room and lead out onto an amazing balcony. The room itself is larger than my flat at home and I could get seriously lost in the biggest bed I have ever seen. The room is immaculate and looks modern and tasteful.

Feeling like an excited girl at Christmas, I run around the room grinning to myself, exploring every inch of the best room I have ever stayed in.

Another door leads into a huge bathroom, all marble and chrome, with the biggest walk in shower and slipper bath. This room also has double doors leading out onto the balcony with the same view of the bay.

This is the best moment of my life. Sad really, but true. I never want to leave this place. I'm in paradise and could live here forever. Maybe the man on reception is my guardian Angel in disguise. At this moment I think I love him because the thought of a whole week living like royalty is one memory I will keep with me forever.

I start to unpack and carefully unfold all of my meticulously packed clothes. I straighten them out on the hangers and stow the suitcase away. My toiletries are lined up precisely in the bathroom in the correct order of use. All the labels are facing forwards and I check for any leakage from the pressure on the aircraft. Everything seems to be intact, so I grab my wet wipes and set about disinfecting the room.

Then I check the bed for any bugs or unmentionables before giving the bathroom a quick wipe - paying particular care to the toilet seat. There! Now I can fully relax, safe in the knowledge everything is exactly as it should be.

I quickly change into a skirt and off the shoulder top and head to Marcus's room.

Let's get this party started.

~*~*~*~*~

Chapter 8

The room is full of the crew and I take a drink from the makeshift bar on the dressing table and grab a spot next to Rachel. I feel smug as I notice that Marcus's room is half the size of mine and nowhere near as opulent. His view is of the street below, not the amazing view of the bay that I am going to enjoy for the next seven nights.

Rachel nudges me and points to Jo.

"Look, she couldn't get further away from Pete if she tried."

I stifle a giggle as I see them at opposite ends of the room. Both looking pointedly away from the other and yet conscious of every move the other one makes. Rachel giggles.

"I'm going to make it my mission to get them back together this trip."

I nod in agreement.

"Yes, this is all silly if you ask me. They are obviously made for each other and could be having a romantic trip away together if they weren't so stubborn."

Jenny comes and sits down next to me on the other side and looks around her fearfully.

"I've got a bad feeling about this place. My room is right in the middle and I have checked the fire escape plan and it would take me longer than most to reach my exit. The only way out appears to be at either end of the corridor and I'm in the middle. The lifts would be out of bounds and I'm right by them. It's too high up to jump to safety and I can't see an easy way out."

Rachel and I share a grin and she says kindly.

"I'm sure it will be fine. This is a five-star hotel and they will have made sure they have every certificate going. I'm sure the sprinkler system is a good one and the alarms would sound in plenty of time if there was even a hint of smoke in the building."

Jenny looks unconvinced.

"But I've heard that people die due to carbon monoxide poisoning in these resorts. What if the silent killer is lurking in the air vents and I never wake up? I can't sleep with the balcony door open because of the midges. They could infect me with lime disease as well as that new one they are all talking about. What's it called?"

"Zika virus." I say, thinking she may have a point.

Rachel looks at us with exasperation.

"Stop it, both of you. Nothing is going to happen except that we are going to have an amazing trip."

Suddenly, we hear Barry shout.

"Remember to check under your beds for bugs. These foreign countries harbour all sorts under them."

I share an agonised look with Jenny as Marcus says loudly.

"He's right. I haven't even checked mine yet. Come on everyone, do me a favour and check under every available surface for me."

The room erupts into a bug searching frenzy and then we hear Jenny's agonised shriek

"AAAARRRGGHHH!"

She jumps on the bed and turns as white as the sheets she's standing on. She stutters,

"Under here. I think there's a snake."

I quickly join her on the bed and Pete races over like a superhero. I feel pure terror fill my whole body as he says in a whisper.

"Nobody move, there is something there."

He reaches under slowly and carefully and you could hear a pin drop in the room. Jo clutches her hand to her chest and looks at him with terror-filled eyes. Then he slowly removes his hand from under the bed and says in a loud voice.

"Got it!"

Then he throws the offending reptile at the terrified crew all jostling for position on the now overcrowded bed.

The screams are off the scale as we all await the inevitable. Pete, Barry, and Marcus however, dissolve into hysterics and we look down at the plastic snake residing innocently on the bed.

Jo screams, "You stupid idiots. How could you think that was a good idea? Look at Jenny, she's ready to die on the spot. You're so immature and don't ever think of the consequences of your actions."

She glares at Pete as she says it and he has the grace to look ashamed as Jenny shivers uncontrollably, tears running down her face.

We pull her down and Rachel and I put our arms around her shoulders.

"It's ok, Jenny. Just the guys being guys. There aren't really any bugs."

Jenny tries to stop but anguished sobs rack her body as the shock takes hold."

Jo glares at Pete with a look that says he should be dead right now.

"Get Jenny a double gin and make it snappy. This is all your fault you stupid idiot. You've ruined a good evening with your stupid prank and Jenny will probably have nightmares because of it."

Pete looks suitably chastened and quickly does as she says.

He hands Jenny the drink and smiles kindly.

"I'm sorry, Jenny. It was just a prank. I didn't think."
Jo snarls. "You never do, imbecile."
Jenny takes a sip of the drink and coughs.
"I'm sorry. I didn't mean to overreact."
Jo just rolls her eyes and the others grab their drinks and carry on chatting. Jenny takes a gulp of air.
"I hate this. I don't know why I'm so anxious all the time. I wish I could shake it off but it's getting worse, not better."
Rachel says gently.
"Well, we're here to help you. This trip is just what you need, and we will make it our mission to help you unwind. Put this unfortunate incident out of your mind and start again. I'll come back to your room later and check it for bugs. We will also map out an escape plan and I will ask at reception when the air conditioning unit was last inspected. You can then sleep well with the knowledge you will wake up in the morning."
Jenny looks at her gratefully and Jo pulls me to one side.
"I could kill Pete. He never thinks. It's always about getting a cheap laugh with him. I wish he had never joined this trip. Look at Jenny. She's been set three steps back because of him. I say we try to avoid him for the rest of the trip."
I nod and let her vent about Pete for the next twenty minutes. This is going to be a long night. I need to get those two back together and fast, for my own sanity's sake.

~*~*~*~*~

Chapter 9

We all head out to grab some dinner. As is typical of these trips we move around enmasse and get lots of strange looks.

I walk with Jo, Jenny, and Rachel and laugh to myself at the daggers Jo throws into Pete's back as he walks on ahead.

We end up at a nice restaurant that appears to specialise in all sorts. There are some waiters on the door who hand us all a shot of tequila to get us on our way. I forgot about this. Tequila shots are like glasses of water here in Mexico. I know they water them down, but you could still get extremely drunk before you've even ordered your starter.

We sit down at a huge table and order our meals. As usual, the drinks are off the scale and it doesn't take long for our table to become extremely raucous.

I love this. Being with my friends on a working holiday. It's why we endure the back-to-back flights to Europe and the twelve-hour days. Every so often we get a trip away which makes it all worthwhile.

Before we grab dessert, there is an almighty racket as the waiters start banging drums and shouting. I watch as they carry a birthday cake through the packed restaurant and stop by our table.

"Who is Meez Rachel?"

We grin and Marcus points Rachel out.

"There she is, the birthday girl."

Rachel turns as red as a Matador's cape as the whole restaurant starts singing *Happy Birthday*. I grin at Marcus as he takes her photo. This is typical. Every night it's

44

someone's turn to be the birthday boy or girl. Nobody knows except the designated chooser - in this case, Marcus.

Rachel grins as we all stuff the gorgeous chocolate cake into our mouths.

"Where are my presents?" Rachel shouts and everyone throws their napkins at her.

The waiter brings another round of tequila shots and we all bang them on the table together and down them in one.

Even Jo is looking happier, although she has positioned herself well away from Pete at the other end of the table. I keep on seeing him look at her with a pained expression and feel sorry for him. I'm sure there's no such person as Margaret but the damage has been done.

Once we head back, it's just time for a nightcap in the crew room before calling it a night.

Finally, I'm alone in my superior room. I take a moment to look at the bay from my balcony. The lights twinkle all around the dark expanse of water and its breathtaking. I wonder if Luke is looking at this same view now. I hope I find him soon because I can't relax until I know he is definitely here. Maybe something will happen with him. I certainly hope so.

It's those thoughts that I take to bed with me in my bed the size of a small country. As I lie width ways - because I can, I drift off into a deep sleep.

The sun peeks in through a crack in the blinds and just for a minute I forget where I am. Then it all comes flooding back and a warm feeling spreads through me. This is it. The first day of a glorious week. Lots of rest and relaxation followed by party nights and bad behaviour. Perfect.

I pull on some shorts and a vest top and make myself look presentable for breakfast. I take extra care in case I see Luke. I can't ignore the feeling of excitement that fills me at the thought of seeing him again. I think I dreamt of him last night because when I woke up I had this warm glow all over me. Either that or the air conditioning unit was playing up.

As soon as I enter the dining room I scan it looking for a familiar face. Ok, I'm shamelessly looking for Luke but then I hear, "Becca, over here."

Looking in the direction the voice is coming from, I smile as I see Rachel and Jenny sitting at a table in the corner.

Taking my seat, I grin at their happy faces.

"This place is amazing, isn't it?"

Rachel nods, her eyes shining.

"You can say that again. I can't believe that we managed to engineer this trip. It's incredibly sought after and everyone always requests it. The fact we all got it is amazing."

Jenny nods.

"Yes, I must have pestered crewing for a month to get on it. I think they did it to stop me from hounding them 24/7."

I sit back and look around, taking in the calm, peaceful atmosphere of the restaurant.

Jenny nods towards the 'help yourself buffet' at one end of the room.

"Who wants to come with me and grab some of that delicious looking food?"

I seize the chance for another scan of the room and smile happily.

"I'll come with you."

Rachel smiles.

"I'll keep our table and look out for Jo. Who knows what trouble she is concocting for poor Pete as we speak?"

Laughing, I follow Jenny to grab some food.

I load up with fruit, pastries, and yoghurts and look around me the whole time. There is no sign of Luke anywhere and I try to push down the feelings of disappointment.

Jenny frowns as she looks at the array of delights in front of us.

"Do you think these are safe to eat? I mean, the fruit may have been washed in the water. It's the golden rule when in a foreign country - don't drink the water or get ice cubes in your drinks due to contamination."

I sigh to myself. Here we go again.

I just smile kindly.

"I think we'll be ok. The fruit is probably natural and hasn't been washed. The pastries should be fine, and the yoghurts are pre-packed. I don't think you can go far wrong with this."

She still looks unconvinced but braves a slice of melon and a sealed pot of yoghurt.

As we head back to the table, I scan the room again and feel mildly irritated that Luke wasn't waiting for me. Come to think of it, I would have expected to have seen him last night waiting around in reception. This happy ever after of mine is not going to plan.

When we get back, I see that Jo has joined us looking absolutely amazing in a pretty sundress. Her hair is swept back, and she looks the epitome of chic. As we sit down, I look at her in admiration.

"Jo, you look amazing. That colour really suits you."

She looks smug.

"It's new. I intend on looking amazing at every opportunity on this trip to wipe all thoughts of Margaret from Pete's mind. By the end of this week, the only name he will want to hear is mine."

Rachel looks interested.

"Have you decided to forgive him then?"

She shakes her head.

"No, not yet. I just want him to see what he's given up. He will regret the day he let that woman into his head when he sees what it's cost him."

Rachel looks at me with a worried expression and I shrug.

"He may be telling the truth though. What if he is and you are giving up on a happy future with the man of your dreams?"

Jo snorts.

"I doubt that. Have any of you ever spoken another man's name when in the throes of passion? I don't think so. In fact, the more I think about it the more I believe it. I didn't think anything when he joined our local Conservative club last month. He's always been a Tory, and I thought he was just doing his civic duty. Maybe he has always harboured a secret crush on Margaret Thatcher."

We all burst out laughing and Jo shakes her head.

"You may laugh but I've heard of this happening all the time. Some men love a dominant woman and there's none more so than the iron lady herself. Perhaps he has always had a fixation for a strong powerful woman and joining the party helped satisfy his need. If you ask me, it's all weird and I'm well out of it."

I quickly stuff a slice of melon in my mouth before I burst out laughing. Jo looks so serious and convinced she is right, despite how ridiculous she sounds.

Jenny sighs heavily.

"I wish I had someone to argue with, let alone call me by another woman's name. I would even be happy with that if it meant I had someone who loved me."

We all look at each other and my heart reaches out to the lost soul in front of me.

Poor Jenny. She has lived with her mum all of her life and to my knowledge has never had a serious boyfriend. They used to do everything together and it must have been devastating when her mum got cancer. Despite her phobias and nervous disposition, Jenny is the sweetest, kindest girl you could ever meet and is a real credit to her mum.

Rachel looks at her kindly. "It must be hard, honey. You aren't alone though. You have the three of us and we won't let you down. You are always welcome to stay at our house and I'm sure in time you will meet a man who will love you more than the moon and stars."

Jenny smiles tremulously. "I hope so. It's all any of us want - isn't it? To find our soul mate and live our lives together as a team. I want that more than anything."

I look at her wistfully.

"We all do, Jenny. When you think of it though, Rachel is the only one of us who has found it so far. We are all in the same boat and the clock is ticking. Well, let's just make sure we make the most of our trip here and who knows what it may bring."

Jo looks thoughtful and Rachel looks - well strange if I'm honest. She looks out to sea and I note her shoulders have slumped and her body language defensive. Something definitely isn't right there. I make a vow to discover what's bothering her because something definitely is.

We carry on with our breakfast and then we hear a terse, "Thanks a lot, Jo."

Looking up, I see a disgruntled Pete standing at our table glaring at Jo. While she looks restful and totally amazing, he looks as if he hasn't slept a wink all night. He hasn't shaved and the black circles underneath his eyes tell of a night without sleep. She smiles at him sweetly.

"Good morning, Peter. I trust you slept well."

She grins as he looks at her angrily.

"Not really. In fact, I think I only got about one hours sleep all night. For some reason I had a wake-up call every hour. It appears that Margaret was waiting for me in the gym, the restaurant, reception, by the pool - you name it, she was there. No prizes for guessing who set up those calls."

Jo just shrugs and looks at him innocently.

"If that's what you want to believe."

Pete looks at her with frustrated eyes. He runs his fingers through his dishevelled hair and growls.

"We need to talk - urgently."

Shaking her head, Jo picks up a piece of papaya and eats it slowly while looking at him innocently. When she finishes, she shrugs.

"I don't think we have anything left to say. Now, if you'll excuse us, Pete, you look as if you need a strong cup of coffee and twelve hours sleep. Don't let us keep you."

He glares at her angrily.

"This isn't over, Jo."

She smiles sweetly.

"Apparently it is. Now off you go and leave me alone."

As he storms off, I feel sorry for him. I look at her with exasperation.

"For goodness' sake, Jo. I believe him. You can tell that the man is at his wit's end. He obviously adores you but if you push him like this, it could fast become the War of the Roses. Why don't you accept that it was a mistake and get back to the loving relationship you had?"

Her eyes fill with tears and I instantly feel bad. She says shakily.

"I wish I could. I want to believe him more than anything, but he hurt me. When you love someone as much as I do him it's hard to hear another woman's name on his lips. What if you're wrong and he is having an affair? He may secretly crave another and I'm just someone he is killing time with. I can't let it go because he has destroyed my soul."

Rachel and Jenny look at me in total shock. This isn't like Jo. She is usually tough and rational. Despite her no-nonsense approach, she is soft and kind. You couldn't wish for a better friend and she is the true definition of loyalty. This must have shocked her to the core, and she is reacting the only way she knows how. I can see how wounded she is and my heart reaches out to her.

Rachel puts her arm around her.

"If it's any consolation, I think Pete is hurting even more than you are. I agree with Becca. I think it was one of those things that happen that makes no sense. Pete adores you, it's obvious. You should let it go and give him the benefit of the doubt."

Just for a moment, I think she is wavering and then I see the fire re-ignite in her eyes.

"Where's the fun in that? No, I fully intend on making him pay. Only when I have brought him to his knees, will I think about forgiveness. Come on, let's go and grab our positions by the pool. I need to soak up the sun's healing rays and distance myself from all thoughts of Pete and Margaret."

Sighing inside, I follow her out.

~*~*~*~*~

Chapter 10

"This is the life."

I nod and look around me at the paradise waiting.

This place is amazing. The pool stretches out before us and appears to fall off the edge into the sea. There is nothing between the end of the pool and the beautiful bay before us. Palm trees sway in the gentle breeze and the opulent cushioned sunbeds line up around the cool, clear water. All in all, it looks like paradise.

Rachel throws her towel down on the nearest one and sighs.

"At last! I fully intend on spending the day on this bed with my book boyfriend. The only time I will put him down is to sip a colourful cocktail or dive into that amazing pool."

She reaches down and pulls her t-shirt over her head and shimmies out of her shorts. After a quick spray of suntan lotion, she dons her huge glasses and snaps open her Kindle. Jenny looks worried - as usual and squints up at the sun.

"I've only got factor 50. Do you think I should grab an umbrella to keep the UV rays away? I mean, I freckle really easily which could develop into a mole. What if I am prone to melanoma and end up sick as a result? Maybe I should stay covered up."

I see Jo's irritated glare and frown her a warning. Jenny has every right to fear cancer after seeing its devastating effects on her mum. Of course, she must feel worried.

I look around and spy a table and chairs nearby.

"I'll help you drag those over here if you like. You can set up camp under the umbrella and we could use the table for our stuff."

She looks at me gratefully.

"Thanks, Becca."

By the time we have secured Jenny in her shady haven, I notice Jo has stretched out looking like a supermodel. She wasn't kidding when she said she was going to show Pete what he was missing. Her bikini alone looks expensive and hugs her curves like a second skin. Her hair gleams brightly and her toenails sparkle with an expensive pedicure. She is certainly attracting some admiring looks and I feel a little envious if I'm honest.

Once everyone is settled, I sort myself out.

I make sure that my towel is neatly secured on the sunbed with no creases. Then I line up my factor 30 and water bottle neatly on the table beside me, right next to the hydrating spray for my face and body and the hair protector spray. My Kindle is placed in front of them and I carefully wipe the smears from my sunglasses. After folding up my canvas bag, neatly, I set about liberally coating myself with sunscreen. Once I am sure that every inch of me is protected, I grab my floppy sunhat and shades and sit back on my sunbed and grab my Kindle. Not that I intend on reading even one word. From my vantage point I can see every inch of this pool area. I fully intend on hiding behind my shades and looking out for Luke for the whole day if necessary.

After one hour of the hot intense sun, I am in serious need of a cooling dip in the pool. This is so frustrating. I wanted Luke to see me looking like a complete goddess when he emerged, taut and toned and desperately seeking me! However, there is still no sign of him and my irritability is off the scale. Jo stretches out with contentment beside me.

"Is anyone up for a dip in the pool? I'm sweating buckets here."

We all spring from our beds like a Jack from a box. Looking glamourous is hard and after one hour I am beaten. We all jump into the pool and as I feel the cold, crystal water soothing my hot body, I feel my skin's relief.

We swim over to the edge of the pool and look out at the bay before us.

"This view is breath-taking."

Rachel sighs dreamily and I nod in agreement.

"It doesn't get much better than this, does it?"

Jenny smiles happily.

"You know, for the first time since my mum died, I feel relaxed. Maybe this was just what I needed. To get away from the stress back at home and forget about it all for the week. It's been so full on; my head has been permanently spinning since it happened. Maybe this week is the start of my new life and far from fearing it, I should welcome it and look forward rather than back."

Jo looks at her with misty eyes.

"Well done, Jenny. That's the attitude. You're right. It's good to leave the trials and tribulations of home back there and just concentrate on healing. I'm with you. I want to forget about the troubles at home and focus on mending my soul."

Rachel sighs heavily.

"Me too."

We look at her in shock and Jo says, somewhat harshly.

"But you're living the dream. What have you got to worry about?"

Rachel looks away and I see the shutters come up.

"Nothing, forget I said anything."

I look at her and wonder what's going on in her life. Surely, she should be living the dream. She's a newlywed and her husband is a gorgeous Italian stallion. They have dated for a couple of years and he absolutely adores her. I wonder what's going on?

By lunchtime, there is still no sign of Luke. I feel strangely upset and unsettled. Surely, he would have emerged by now. This hotel may be big, but everyone comes to the pool on their first day, don't they?

The pool area is busy but not busy enough that I wouldn't be able to see him. I see that Pete and Barry have tucked themselves away from us on the opposite side of the pool. Every time Jo gets in the pool, Pete gets out and I feel frustrated at their childish behaviour. Jenny has calmed down and appears happier and Rachel has been reading for most of the day. Feeling disgruntled I decide to have a little sleep and rest my eyes. Laying on my front I drift off to sleep feeling the gentle caress of the sun's rays on my back.

I'm not sure how long I slept for before I hear a man's voice saying loudly.

"Found you."

I lift my head and am faced with the sight of a mans crowded set of white Speedos right in front of my face. With a start, I sit up and blink, trying to focus on the person standing at the top of my sunbed. As I raise my eyes my stomach lurches as I see the gaze of First Class man, raking my near naked body with his predatory eyes.

I shiver as he licks his lips and says in a low voice.

"I was hoping to run into you. This is a happy coincidence. We can keep each other company."

I feel the startled gazes of my friends as they take in the scene and I'm lost for words. This can't be happening.

Quickly, I grab my sarong and drape it over my body and don't miss the disappointment in his eyes.

Shaking my head, I stutter.

"Oh, yes, hi. What a coincidence. I'm sorry but I'm with my friends. Um, strictly a male free zone unless you count Marcus who is allowed as an honorary female."

I see Rachel stifling a giggle as the passenger looks surprised.

"Four lovely ladies like you shouldn't be on your own. How about you make me the exception to the rule?"

I shake my head in horror.

"No, sorry. We have strict rules about mixing with our passengers. It's um against the laws of the airlines. In fact, we may even lose our jobs if we're found out."

He looks shocked.

"Really? That's harsh. Well, I won't tell if you won't. How about I just sit over there and when you're ready we can grab a drink somewhere private?"

I feel the bile rising in my throat as I take in the sight of his skin-tight swimwear failing to disguise his interest. He is staring at me with such a look of pure lust that I feel violated.

Jo speaks up abruptly.

"Listen, back off. We are trying to enjoy a nice relaxing few days away from the stresses of work and men. If Becca wants to meet up with you she will. If she says no, then take the hint and do one."

We all look at her in shock and the passenger looks at us angrily.

He turns on his heels and says bitterly.

"Your loss. Bloody lesbians."

As he stomps off, I look at the others in shock.

"Did that just really happen?"

Rachel laughs out loud and wipes a tear from her eye.

"Did you see what he was wearing? I haven't seen anything like it since the seventies."

Jenny giggles.

"Who wears white Speedos these days? The man was deluded if he ever thought that would interest you."

Jo snorts. "Pervert. What gives people like him the right to come and make a girl feel uncomfortable. Waking up with that thrust in your face was enough to put anyone off - even Marcus."

I shake my head.

"I don't know about that. Where is he by the way?"

Jenny nods towards the cocktail bar on the other side of the pool.

"He's been propping that up for the last hour talking to the bartender. If I'm not mistaken, he's been flirting his way through several Pina Coladas."

Looking over, I see Marcus laughing at something the dishy Mexican bartender is saying and I roll my eyes.

"Typical Marcus."

Pulling my sarong tightly around me, I head off to find him.

He sees me coming and smiles happily.

"Becca, my darling. Come and grab a cocktail and tell me what's happening."

I climb onto the stool beside him and smile at the rather hot guy behind the bar.

"Just a pineapple juice please."

Marcus rolls his eyes. "You lightweight, Becca."

He takes a sip of his coloured drink and smiles happily.

"Oh my god, Becca. This place is amazing. I've had so much fun already and planned our whole trip already with Elvis the concierge."

I look at him with interest.

"Why, what have you planned?"

He grins and taps his nose.

"All in good time darling girl. Well, for starters, Elvis told me that the Great Ernesto is due to visit the hotel bar for a show."

I grin.

"The Great Ernesto? Who's he when he's at home?"

Marcus lowers his voice.

"Apparently, he's a hypnotist. A good one at that. Elvis told me it's hilarious at what he can get people to do."

I look at him sharply.

"And what are your plans?"

He looks at me innocently.

"Nothing. I just thought we would pay a visit and see for ourselves. After that, we can hit the English bar along the strip. They say it's the place to be in Acapulco and the tequila shots never stop coming. If you want a great night out, that's the place to start."

Laughing, I grab my drink and lower my voice.

"Hey, you haven't seen Luke anywhere have you?"

Marcus grins and his eyes dance with amusement.

"Dirty girl. All you want is an eyeful of that sex god in his next to nothing. Well, I'm with you on that. But to answer your question I haven't had so much of a whiff that he's in this hotel. Mark my words though, if he's here I'll soon sniff him out."

Rolling my eyes, I head back to the others trying to push down the feeling of pure desperation that's beginning to consume me. Where is he?

~*~*~*~*~

Chapter 11

"A hypnotist! I'll believe that when I see it."

We are all waiting in the lobby for the others to arrive and Jo looks at me with a bored expression.

"Those acts are so lame. Full of an audience of planted people to give the impression that he is kosha. Sounds like a nightmare to me."

Shrugging, I look around the reception once again for Luke. This is starting to become a habit. I'm on edge all the time and it's ruining this whole trip.

Jo looks thoughtful.

"It may be interesting in some ways though."

I groan inwardly. No prizes for guessing what's on her mind. Poor Pete.

Rachel and Jenny soon join us, and Jenny looks worried.

"I'm not sure we should be anywhere near a hypnotist. What if we get affected by his hypnotising rays? It could completely mess with our heads."

Jo rolls her eyes and Rachel grins.

"It's all pretend, Jenny. It's just a show and done to entertain. We will be perfectly safe."

By the time the rest of the crew join us I'm feeling like offering myself up to be hypnotised. I need to erase every thought of Luke from my brain before I self-destruct.

Marcus claps his hands.

"Right then bitches. It's time to step into the mystical, magical world of the unknown. What we will experience tonight will change our lives forever. Now, remember, what goes on in Acapulco stays in Acapulco. If any of you think you're a horse or a rabbit by the end of the night, no photos on Instagram of Facebook. It will be our little secret."

Giggling, we all follow him into the Bar.

The Bar is crowded, and it takes some doing to grab a table. Due to the size of our party we have to spread out, which is probably a good thing. There is a small stage at the end with a silver curtain and spotlights trained on a man getting his act together.

We order some drinks and once again, I scan the room for a sighting of Luke. All I manage to see is the First-Class passenger, pressed against a poor unfortunate woman near the Bar. At least he's moved on which fills me with considerable relief.

Jo looks around and frowns as she sees Pete laughing with Caitlyn at another table. Rachel nudges me and pulls a face.

"She's a nightmare. She's treated him so badly and yet still gets jealous when he talks to another woman. Even Caitlyn, who is married to a car mechanic from Weybridge and expecting her first baby."

I roll my eyes. "What are we going to do with her?"

Rachel grins. "I'm sure they will work it out."

Before I'm tempted to ask what's bothering her, we hear the shrill shriek of the microphone as the Great Ernesto taps it to test that it's working. He clears his throat and shouts.

"Ladies and gentlemen. Welcome to the unexplained. I am the great Ernesto and am here to show you the power of the mind. What you will see will amaze you, dazzle you and change your lives forever. You will not believe your eyes and talk about it for eternity. Ladies and gentlemen, prepare to be hypnotised."

Marcus claps his hands and looks excited.

"Oh my god, this is so exciting. I hope he chooses me."

Jenny looks worried and Rachel giggles.

"If Jo's got any say in it, he'll choose Pete."

Looking over, I see her looking thoughtful and Pete looking slightly nervous. This could be interesting.

We watch as the great one points to a man in the second row and beckons him up. He then proceeds to look deeply into his eyes and swings some sort of medallion in front of his face.

Jo snorts.

"Oh, for goodness' sake, how cliched. This is like some cheap show at a holiday camp."

She takes a swig of her wine and looks around with a bored expression.

We all watch as the man starts clucking like a chicken and disappears off into the audience, strutting like he has wings. My heart sinks. Jo's right, this show is lame.

The next victim is a woman who is convinced into believing she's an opera singer. That is fairly amusing as she can't sing for toffee but believes she's amazing. We're all in fits as she sings at the top of her voice, completely out of tune as the man chicken struts around her.

He then scans the crowd and picks another man to come forward who is skulking at the back.

His friends start howling with laughter as the man is hypnotised into believing he is God's gift to women. We all watch as he sidles up to the nearest woman and starts flirting with her outrageously.

I am now starting to enjoy myself watching these people make complete fools of themselves. Even if it is a hoax, it's very funny.

Then to our complete and utter amazement, he calls up his next victim and we watch in total shock as Jenny climbs onto the small stage.

Rachel grabs my arm and Jo breathes in heavily.

"Oh my God, what is she doing?"

We watch as if frozen as Jenny cowers before him and whispers something in his ear. He nods and then addresses the audience.

"This is the brave Jenny. She has told me that she holds much fear in her heart. It is consuming her and stifling her ability to live a normal life. Jenny needs our help to drive the fear from her body and mind. Silence, ladies and gentlemen, Jenny needs to embrace the power of the mind."

Suddenly, you could hear a pin drop and the lights change to a ghostly blue. Rachel whispers, "We should stop her."

I shake my head as Jo says softly, "Leave her, this may be just what she needs."

We watch and listen as the Great Ernesto waves his medallion from side to side in front of Jenny's eyes. He speaks in a calm, soft voice.

"Jenny, feel the fear leave your body. Watch it tick away with the movement of time. Watch it go and feel the release. Every swing of the pendulum will take a little more away. Open your mind to a future with no fear. All the things you fear are locked on the wind of change. Watch them go my brave Jenny. Say goodbye to them because they will never return. You are strong. Feel the strength fill your mind and body and repeat after me - I am strong."

Jenny watches the moving medallion and says in a clear, strong voice. "I am strong."

He says.

"Louder my angel. I want to hear you shout."

She shouts louder.

"I am strong."

He says in a loud voice.

"Watch the fear disappear. Everyone shout, 'You are strong,' to Jenny."

The audience starts to shout the words and Jenny joins in. We watch as she starts screaming, "I am strong," all the time watching the medallion swing.

Ernesto holds up his hand and the room falls silent. He says in a strong voice.

"Relinquish your fear, Jenny. There is nothing to fear but fear itself. Banish the fear and let the light in. Do you relinquish the fear, Jenny?"

She shouts.

"Yes, I have no fear."

Then he closes his hand around the medallion and clicks his fingers. Jenny's head snaps up, and she looks at him in astonishment. He says in a strong voice.

"How do you feel, Jenny?"

She looks around at the audience, her eyes wide. Shaking her head, she looks at everyone in complete astonishment.

As she stands up a huge smile breaks out across her face.

"I feel amazing. I feel liberated and happy. It's as if a huge weight has shifted from inside me and I feel light and carefree."

The audience starts clapping and cheering and I look at the others in total astonishment.

"What just happened?"

Rachel looks worried.

"I hope she'll be ok. What if he's messed with her mind?"

Jo looks thoughtful.

"Even if he has, it may be in a good way. Maybe this is just what she needed to shake off her fears. Who knows, our little Jenny may have just changed her life forever."

~*~*~*~*~

Chapter 12

Three shots of tequila later at the English bar on the strip, and I'm beginning to believe that Jenny has indeed changed her life. Apparently, the old Jenny has been left on that hypnotist's stage and the new Jenny is out of control.

As soon as we set foot inside this place, she was in the thick of it. So far, she has entered a drinking competition and knocked back the tequila as if it's water. She's had a bucket of water dumped all over her in a wet t-shirt contest and now it appears she is playing *pass the mango* in a chain of extremely willing, drunken men. Jo looks at us with amazement.

"Wow, new Jenny is a lot of fun. She is having the time of her life and I want what she's having. Who'd have thought that guy was the real deal."

Marcus grins after snapping yet another picture of Jenny to torture her with when she snaps out of it.

"Actually, the guy is a dud. I cornered him afterwards, and he said his real name is Ernest Smith from Hartlepool. He's just doing the circuit out here and those other people are his employees. Jenny believed in him and her mind has switched all by itself. He said he's seen it before. If someone really wants to believe something, it only takes the power of self-belief to re-focus the brain. That is Jenny up there and she just needed to believe in herself."

Rachel shakes her head in astonishment.

"Wow, that's amazing. If I hadn't seen it myself, I would never have guessed. I hope she doesn't wake up tomorrow and forget about it. She's having the time of her life over there."

We watch as Jenny leads the mango line in a conga around the bar. She is laughing, and her eyes are sparkling and not just with the effects of the tequila. Maybe this is her grief taking her down a different path. They say that grief does the strangest things to you, which is obviously true in her case.

Before long she staggers over and thumps Jo on the back.

"Hey, girlfriend. Do you fancy going skinny dipping? My friends over there said they're up for it, if you guys are."

I stifle a giggle at the horror on Jo's face as she looks over at the drunken crowd of men, all throwing us suggestive looks. Then I see her focus on Pete's absolutely furious one and a wicked glint sparks in her eyes.

"Sure, why not? I'm up for it if you are."

Rachel and I exchange a look of horror as Jenny squeals.

"Yay!! Come on then." She then starts singing,

♫ *It's getting hot in here,
let's take off all our clothes* ♫

Grabbing hold of Jo's hand, she pulls her from the bar and Marcus follows laughing loudly. Rachel looks at me in horror as we quickly follow them out.

We almost have to run to catch up with them as they run shrieking to the beach. Jenny starts pulling her clothes from her body and leaving them in a trail behind her. The guys from the bar follow suit and I start to get extremely worried. One of the guys grabs Jenny and throws her into the sea and her loud shriek of joy bounces all around the bay. Jo quickly jumps in, in her underwear and there is a lot of splashing and shrieks of laughter. Marcus, the dirty boy, takes off all his clothes including his underwear and jumps into the middle of the water party. Rachel looks at me with tears running down her face.

"Come on, if you can't beat them, join them."

I shake my head as a furious Pete races over with Barry.

"What the hell's going on? This is out of control. Stop her, Becca, she's making a complete fool of herself. She could get into all kinds of trouble with those guys."

I share his concern but something about the pure joy bouncing across the water calls to me. Maybe this is what the doctor ordered for us all. One night of pure and utter chaos, throwing caution to the wind. As Rachel starts stripping off her clothes, I join her.

I laugh as I see Pete's shocked expression as we race off into the sea.

Soon we are thrashing around with the rest of them. We engage in a massive water fight and laugh at the sight of Marcus wrestling with the drunk guys in a play fight. Then they turn their attention to us. We each find ourselves hauled onto the shoulders of a near naked man as we try to topple each other. It doesn't take Pete long to wade in and try to dislodge Jo from the shoulders of a tattooed man from Wigan. She is having none of it though and kicks out at him, drenching him in the process. Before long he gives in and just sits on the edge of the beach moodily, while we have the time of our lives.

It doesn't take long before we are exhausted and haul ourselves from the water and grab our clothes. Despite being wet we quickly dress and head back to the bar. The drunk guys are actually really good fun and just intent on topping up their alcohol levels and having a good time.

They are no threat to us and we enjoy having the most fantastic party night that I can ever remember having.

The only dampener is Pete, who sits moodily in the corner, throwing anguished looks towards Jo who couldn't care less. Even Barry joins in as we indulge in a, *pass the mango*, Olympics.

It must be 2 am when we drag ourselves back to the hotel.

By the time I let myself into my superior room the euphoria from the alcohol is wearing off. As I wander through the large room all alone I sink into a pit of despair.

This is it. As usual, I am all alone and probably will be forever. Becca the lush has made an appearance and will probably dictate my future. I am destined to always return alone and get my kicks from frolicking with naked men in the sea.

Pushing my way out onto the balcony, I look at the beautiful lights twinkling all around Acapulco Bay.

I have never felt so alone. My loneliness is consuming me and so I do what I have always done when I feel at my lowest point. As I lean on my balcony, I start to sing in a sad and small voice.

♪*Can you hear the drums, Fernando?*
I remember long ago another starry night like this♪

I sniff and carry on, slightly louder.

♪*In the firelight, Fernando.*
You were humming to yourself and softly strumming your guitar.
I could hear the distant drums and sounds of bugle calls were coming from afar♪

Just as I'm about to ramp up the volume for the chorus I hear a discreet cough from the balcony next to me.

Spinning towards the sound, I try to focus on the shadowy figure who appears to be stalking me in the early hours of the morning. Shakily, I say in what I think is a forceful voice,

"Who is it?"

They move into the light and my heart threatens to burst inside me as Luke emerges from the shadows.

I must be hallucinating and blink several times to unscramble my brain.

He smiles that devastating, female kryptonite, smile and my whole-body sighs.

"Sorry to interrupt. I thought it was you."

Shaking my head from side to side like a mad woman, I stutter.

"What... how... when.... why... who?"

He grins, and I pant with desire.

"It appears that we are neighbours."

Trying to will my mouth to join the rest of my body from its new position on the floor, I am suddenly acutely aware that I'm looking my worst. In fact, I have probably never looked worse. My makeup has run down my face from the effects of the sea frolic and I'm wet through. My dress is now clinging to my body like a wet rag and is probably every man's fantasy as it exposes my curves through the sheer fabric. My hair is wet and bedraggled and my eyes probably bloodshot from the tequila. Far from looking like a goddess, I expect I look like a hoe.

Luke, however, looks good enough to eat. His hair is spiky on top and begging for my fingers to rifle through it. He is wearing a figure-hugging t-shirt and combat shorts and his feet are bare. He looks sleepy and slightly vulnerable and it takes what is left of my inner strength not to launch myself on him like a heat-seeking missile.

He smiles softly.

"I was hoping to run into you. The trouble is, things took a turn for the worse after I checked in and I haven't left my room since arriving."

I look at him in shock.

"What happened?"

He laughs softly.

"It appears that I've been given the honeymoon suite and everything that goes with it. When I arrived, there was a feast of oysters laid out for my pleasure, alongside a bottle of champagne. I was tired from the flight so decided to polish off the lot on my heart-shaped, rose petal strewn bed while watching the football. Next thing I know, I was revisiting the oysters in the bathroom and must have passed out from the effects of the champagne. I spent all night and all of today recovering from a huge dose of food poisoning and it's only now that I feel human again."

I look at him with concern.

"Wow, that's rotten luck."

He leans on the rail next to me and looks out at the bay.

"It looks beautiful though. So, tell me, did I miss much?"

He laughs as he says it and I realise just what a mess he must be looking at. I smile shyly.

"Not really, same old things."

He laughs and even in the darkness I notice his eyes twinkle.

"Well, it looks as if I've missed out on quite a night. Maybe you could let me tag along tomorrow and show a guy how to have a good time on his honeymoon without a bride."

I laugh like a madwoman and will myself to tone it down. Gosh, I'm not making a very good impression.

He smiles sweetly.

"Listen, you look as if you need a hot shower. You're shivering despite the fact it's 20 degrees in the middle of the night. Why don't you make yourself comfortable and I'll fetch you a hot drink to warm you up? We could watch the sunrise together, unless you would rather go to sleep that is."

As if. I'm suddenly more awake than I've ever been in my life. What, sleep during the best moment of my life? He has got to be kidding.

I smile, trying to look nonchalant as if things like this happen to me every day.

"That sounds great. Just give me five minutes and I'll be back."

He smiles, and my heart does a Triple Axel.

As I rush towards my bathroom, I break every rule I possess. I throw my sodden clothes to the ground and don't even attempt to pick them up, rinse them and hang them neatly to dry. Then, I frantically scrub every inch of me, without following the correct bathing routine that I have adhered to since I was a teenager.

I drag the brush through my hair without a care for split ends and then worry what on earth I should wear. Going against every rule of OCD, I tear through my wardrobe like a hurricane. Clothes are flung from their hangers and quickly rejected as I search for the perfect outfit. It needs to shout, chic, elegant woman, who is poised and sophisticated. Not the inebriated lush that dresses like a tramp that I was five minutes ago.

With a quick squirt of Jo Malone and a five-minute makeover to my face, I take a deep breath and glide back onto the balcony.

~*~*~*~*~

Chapter 13

Luke is leaning over the balcony looking like the sex god that he is. I try to appear cool and chic and lean against the railing in a similar pose. He smiles and looks at me appreciatively.

"You look lovely, Becca."

Willing myself not to burst into loud giggly laughter and do a strange sort of happy clappy dance in front of him, I just smile mysteriously like a woman of the world.

"Oh, this old thing. I forgot I had it with me, really."

I am dressed in a clingy pale blue dress that I have been told suits my womanly curves. My make-up matches and I'm hoping the scent of my Jo Malone is drawing him in. He reaches behind him and offers me a steaming mug of something that smells like hot chocolate.

"Here you go. This should warm you up inside."

Taking the mug gratefully, I take a sip. I feel the kick of the alcohol and slightly worry about my alcohol levels. However, this drink is the tastiest thing that has ever passed my lips- almost as tasty as the man who gave it to me.

I smile and raise my mug to his.

"Cheers, this is just what the doctor ordered."

He laughs softly.

"Yes, I've whipped up this recipe many times on my cold and lonely nights at sea."

Ooh, now I'm even more interested.

"So, what do you do then?"

He looks out towards the bay and says in a low voice.

"I'm a submariner. I work on a submarine for most of the year."

I look at him in surprise.

"Well, that's unexpected. How long have you done that for?"

"Three years. I joined as a weapon engineer officer and have been all over the world. Not that I've seen any of it mind you."

He laughs as I say,

"A bit like me really. I fly in the sky and you fly beneath the sea."

He laughs.

"How long have you been a stewardess?"

"Ten years this month."

He looks impressed.

"That's a lot of air miles."

Grinning, I take another sip of the intoxicating drink.

"It's been good. I've met many friends and enjoyed some amazing trips all around the world. It's come at a cost though."

I feel his scrutiny and instantly regret my big mouth opening, as he says, "Why?"

Mentally, I kick myself as I try to cover up my mistake.

"Oh, you know, always away and never any time to make a life for myself. Most of my friends are married off and I have nothing in common with them anymore."

He looks thoughtful.

"I can relate to that. There aren't many marriages on a submarine. Sometimes we are away for months and that would be hard for any relationship."

An awkward silence descends on us and we both look out to sea as if the answer to everything lies in the bay.

After a few minutes, Luke says softly.

"Listen, Becca, say no if you want, I completely understand but would you like to come and sit over here to watch the sunrise? It may be more comfortable than leaning on the railings and we could sit on the comfy seats instead."

I take a deep breath before I answer. I don't want to shout, *yes* and leap across the balcony like spider woman, so I try to look thoughtful and just smile.

"Oh, that's fine. What shall I do, come and knock on your door?"

He smiles and my heart melts.

"I'll meet you at the door."

Trying not to run, I take my mug and walk inside. Quickly, I check my appearance and remove any smudges under my eyes. I smooth my dress down and take a good few deep breaths. Fantasy evening about to come true. Prayers and wishes been answered, and Father Christmas is obviously real.

I meet Luke at his door which is opposite mine. He smiles and opens the door wider.

"Welcome to my Love Palace, neighbour."

Feeling a little self-conscious, I follow him into the honeymoon suite.

Love Palace is right - wow and double wow!

I stare around at what must be considered romance in Mexico.

The walls are painted red and there are cherubs everywhere. There is even a large mural of naked women and cherubs reclining near a fountain. Mirrors line the ceiling and in the middle, is a massive heart shaped bed with red satin sheets. The bed is littered with rose petals and I swear I saw it move. Great white pillars stand in the middle of the room like a scene from the roman empire and soft shag pile rugs are like heaven to my feet. I look around in total awe and Luke laughs.

"Impressive, isn't it?"

I look around in astonishment and laugh softly.

"This room is like a brothel. Not that I know what one look like of course."

I feel myself turn as red as the sheets as Luke laughs loudly.

"My thoughts exactly. Although, like you, I wouldn't know."

I raise my eyes and look at him pointedly and he grins.

Shaking my head, I take another look around the room as I wander through the Love Palace. I am stunned. This place is everything I would hate to find on my honeymoon. I look at the rose covered bed and shudder. Luke looks at me with interest and I smile.

"These petals would seriously annoy me. Not only would they stain the sheets, but they would end up sticking to you. I expect you will be finding them for the next year in places you forgot you had."

Luke laughs as I blush even further. I must stop talking - immediately!

He nods towards the bathroom.

"It doesn't get any better in there."

Grinning, I head towards the bathroom and do a double take as I open the door. Inside is a bath for two and a huge double shower. Like the bedroom it's fashioned in marble and looks like a scene from the Borgias. Naked paintings and marble statues showcasing various erogenous zones provide the art in the room. The mirror on the ceiling is in the worst possible taste.

Trying to shake the image of myself and Luke in the bath together from my mind, I look at him and laugh.

"Well, this is interesting."

Luke grins as I step into the empty bath and stretch out.

"Hm, I could actually get used to a bath this size."

He smiles and then says firmly,

"Wait there."

I watch him disappear and in no time, he is back with a bottle of champagne and some strawberries. He jumps into the bath and lies the opposite end and hands me a glass of champagne.

"Let's have a bath party. Champagne and strawberries and a crash course in each other's lives."

Grinning, I take the glass and help myself to the strawberries.

Leaning back, I savour the sight of him at my feet and picture us like this forever.

He presses something on the wall and the blinds move at the window and suddenly we can see the bay outside.

He smiles.

"Perfect. We can see the sun rise from here."

I scoot down to his end of the bath and sit beside him facing the view. He clinks my glass to his. "So, tell me everything about yourself, Becca."

I smile but feel a little anxious. He will be so disappointed when he hears about my boring life. I take a deep breath.

"There's not much to tell, really. I live with Malcolm my potted plant in a flat near the airport. I have a sister who is married with a family. I am now an Aunt to Dolly and Ralph and they live near my parents in Milton Keynes. Despite everyone's best attempts, I am still single and have devoted my life to my work. What about you?"

I quickly take a gulp of champagne while I wait with bated breath for his potted history.

"I am thirty-three and live at sea with a bunch of smelly men and a few mad women. When I'm not travelling under the sea, I go home to my parents' house who live in Wiltshire. I have a brother as you know, who was jilted at the altar and a sister who works as a nurse.

Like you, I have resisted their attempts to marry me off to absolutely anyone they can think of. One day I hope to settle down and have a family of my own, but that just seems like something in my distant future. I am here because they wanted me to have a nice break before I head back to sea at the end of the month."

Silence stretches between us as we digest each other's words. I feel crushed. All of my hopes and dreams of a future with the gorgeous man beside me are sailing away under the ocean. How could anything ever work between us? If he wanted to that was. After all, we have just met, and he is probably just being friendly. Just my luck. The man of my dreams with the job of my nightmares.

As the sun rises over the horizon, I gaze at it in wonder. Luke pulls me from the bath and we venture out onto the balcony.

The view is breath-taking.

I say, softly. "Wow."

Luke laughs.

"Yes, wow indeed. You don't get to see many sunrises under the ocean."

I turn and find him looking at me with a strange look in his eyes. Almost lost and wistful. My heart thumps as we share a look. Two strangers wanting the same things by all account. Both locked in a world with no escape, wanting to find that special someone. Maybe destiny had a hand in putting us both here and something could work out between us. The trouble is, we will both be strangers again in a few short days when the return flight arrives.

It may be best not to start something we can't finish. We should just stay friends for both our sakes. I didn't order a broken heart this week and I can see one heading my way if I allow myself to get carried away by the man in front of me.

Once again, my life sucks.

~*~*~*~*~

Chapter 14

By the time the sun rises we are the best of friends. We chat about everything we can to delay the inevitable parting of the ways. It must be 8 am before we hear a knock on the door and Luke grins.

"If I'm not mistaken, this is my breakfast. When you're on your honeymoon it appears that you get breakfast in bed."

He heads to the door and I watch in amazement as a waiter wheels in a trolley laden with breakfast items. The man winks at me and I suddenly feel very self-conscious.

Luke tips the man and jumps onto the bed that wobbles precariously.

He grins, "Waterbed. It takes some getting used to, but it's quite comfortable, really. You should try it."

Grinning, I sit on the edge gingerly and laugh as it wobbles underneath me. Luke laughs and pulls me down beside him and we stare up at ourselves in the mirrored ceiling.

We burst out laughing at the sight and I grin.

"Imagine who has laid here before us and looked at themselves in that mirror. I'm betting they were wearing considerably fewer clothes."

Luke raises his eyes as I blush. My mouth needs a zip, how embarrassing.

He shivers. "Yuk, imagine that. You know, this bed is obviously the sex bed. Countless people have used this bed for their own pleasure; it goes with the territory of the honeymoon suite."

Suddenly, I am very grateful for the layer of clothing separating myself from the sheets.

Luke laughs and pulls me up.

"Come on, you can share my breakfast. Then we can head down to the pool and sleep off the night before."

As I join him I feel considerably brighter than I did yesterday. Even if we're just friends, that's good enough for me.

After breakfast, we decide to head down to the pool to catch up with the others.

I quickly rush back to my room to change and look around with disbelief. I forgot that I trashed my room last night and the sight of the devastation brings my anxiety to the fore. Fighting the urge to restore order to my life I am torn between not missing a minute more of Luke than I have to against giving in to my OCD. My heart wins and I try to blank out the mess as I just quickly grab my sexiest bikini and sarong. I grab hold of my flip flops and glasses and am good to go. It must only be five minutes later that I rush out to meet him.

We surface from our respective rooms at the same time and my heart does a somersault as I stare into those mesmerising eyes. He grins, and I try to focus on not giggling like a schoolgirl and blushing profusely. Instead, I just smile with what I think is a mysterious look but must look like I'm a total idiot to a normal human being like Luke.

We head downstairs and I pretend we are on holiday together. By the time we hit the pool area we have just enjoyed our silver wedding in my mind.

I must be so wrapped up in my deliberations that I don't notice that things have changed considerably since yesterday. Luke, of course, wouldn't know and as we move outside we are greeted by a man with a clipboard.

"About time, darlings."

I notice him looking us up and down and nodding approvingly.

"Good, good, you'll do perfectly. Now, we've reserved your position on the far side of the pool. Set up there and then lie on your beds and wait for further instructions."

I look at Luke in shock and he looks as puzzled as I am as we take in the sight before us.

All around the pool are various cameras and lighting equipment. The pool looks the same but there are considerably fewer beds and it almost looks like someone's own private pool. Even the bar has been shielded by what appears to be a backdrop and there are people milling around everywhere looking as busy as can be.

Luke whispers. "This is strange. Was it like this yesterday?"

I shake my head.

"No, it was just your normal run of the mill pool area. Do you think they know we're just guests because if I'm not mistaken this looks like a film set?"

Luke nods.

"I agree. Maybe we should tell them we're in the wrong place."

Before I can answer a woman rushes up.

"Hurry up, we're running behind. You need to go and lie over there and wait for further instructions."

I open my mouth to explain but Luke nudges me and I see a wicked gleam in his eyes.

"Fine, come on Becca. Let's do as we're told."

I follow him in surprise and he laughs softly, whispering,

"Come on, it'll be fun. It's their mistake and we might never get another chance like this."

I say quietly.

"What do you think it is?"

He shrugs. "Looks like a film or a TV programme. I expect we're a couple of extras. All we probably need to do is lie there in the background."

He grins, and I can't help but be caught up in his excitement. He's right, things like this don't happen every day and it will be fun, something to look back on when I'm older and still alone.

We head over to the far side of the pool and deposit our stuff. As usual, I place my towel carefully on the bed and set out my belongings in order of use. Luke watches me and smirks as the woman rushes over.

"No products are to be visible. We can't advertise anything so put them away."

I look in surprise as she grabs my neatly placed toiletries and bundles them into a bag. She whips my carefully placed towel away and thrusts a large cushion on the bed instead.

She looks us up and down and then says briskly, "Ok, lie on the beds facing each other. The actors will be here soon, and we will make a start. Just do what you would normally do and don't make a sound."

She rushes off and Luke shrugs as he leaps onto his sunbed.

"Fine by me. All I want is to catch up on some sleep, anyway."

Eyeing up the cushion, I wish that she had left my towel. Who knows who has laid their sweaty body on that before me. Gingerly, I lower myself and lie back in what I hope is a sexy pose. If I'm about to be immortalised on film, I want to look my best. Luke, of course, has nothing to worry about. He couldn't get much hotter if he tried. I can't take my eyes off his stomach rippling underneath the muscles and the ink on his chest straining against them. I try not to look at his body, but I am human after all. He must work out a lot!

I watch as he dons his shades and leans back, his hands behind his head and I sigh inwardly. Perfection like that has no business lying beside me. How did I get so lucky to have his brother jilted on his wedding day? It's as if the gods are looking down favourably on me from heaven. Either that or my faithful child companion Blackie the cat who died when I was fifteen. He is the only one who could be looking out for me in the afterlife because so far so good, none of my family have died yet. Even both sets of grandparents are still going strong. I must have good genes.

I try to lie still but find myself fidgeting and feeling extremely curious. I can hear movement all around me and know that filming has begun. I daren't look in case I ruin the 'take' but the curiosity is overwhelming.

I hear gentle murmurs carrying across the pool area towards us but otherwise, there is silence. I think Luke must be asleep because he is so quiet, I daren't look in case I ruin the scene.

It must be five minutes later we hear a loud - "Cut."

Then somebody shouts on some sort of megaphone.

"You, over the far side. It doesn't look right. We need some action over there."

I sit up and look around me and realise he is shouting at us. The woman rushes over and thrusts a bottle of suntan lotion at Luke and says hurriedly.

"Rub this into her. It will look good and give him the action he needs."

Luke grins as he takes the bottle and I feel a hot flush creeping over my body at the thought of his hands on my skin. Cocking his head, he looks at me thoughtfully.

"Hm, this could be interesting."

I blush and then lie quickly back down as the man with the megaphone barks, "Hurry up, we haven't got all day."

We hear him shout, 'action' and then I wait with bated breath. This could end up being extremely embarrassing.

Then I feel Luke's strong hands start rubbing my back. I hold my breath because they are doing unmentionable things to my insides. I try to focus on a lizard that is running around under a neighbouring sunbed. Normally the sight of that would freak me out but nothing and I mean nothing, is going to ruin this fantasy moment for me. All I can feel are his strong hands massaging my skin and nothing has ever felt so good. Now I know I'm in paradise. This is the best moment of my life and I only wish I could film it for my own private collection. I will need this memory on the dark days when I am home in my bachelorette flat for one and a plant.

I suppose it must be a combination of the warmth of the sun and the healing hands of Luke because I can't stop myself and groan as he moves lower down my back. Suddenly, we hear a terse, "No groaning over there. Only the actors can groan."

I hear Luke laugh softly and bury my face in the suspect sweat cushion with embarrassment. Did I really just groan out loud?

Luke whispers.

"Did you just groan, Becca?"

I feel my cheeks flame as I hiss.

"Of course not. You just um… caught a tense spot… um… and my muscles spasmed. Yes… that's it, muscle spasmation."

Luke laughs softly.

"Spasmation. Is that a medical term?"

I can hear the amusement in his voice and stifle a giggle as I squeeze my eyes shut, trying to block out my most embarrassing moment ever. I notice that he carries on though-luckily. I would kick myself if my groaning antics caused his hands to leave my body.

His hands carrying on massaging my back and it feels like heaven. I open my eyes and turn my head towards the other side of the pool. From behind my shades, I get a good view of what is going on. I can see several 'actors' all lying on similar beds to ours. Most appear to be doing the same things, except a few that the cameras are trained on.

As my eyes adjust to the scene, I feel the shock radiating through my body as I see what they are doing. It appears that there is some kind of mass orgy going on in broad daylight. Naked women are sitting astride equally naked men who are doing a lot more than groaning. What the hell?!

I feel tense and quickly turn my head the other way facing the sea. O my god - a porno! Luke and I are acting in a porno movie and now the whole world will see my face. My parents will probably see my picture on the advertising billboards that will spring up all around the world and wonder at the morality of their eldest daughter.

Luke carries on oiling me up and must notice my tense body because he leans down and whispers, "Just look away Becca. Pretend they aren't there."

How can I pretend I'm not in a porno? This is going from the best day of my life to the worst. How humiliating.

The only plus point is that Luke's hands are all over me - legitimately.

I suppose I can put up with being a sex siren if it gives me a few more moments of shoulder rubbing. I feel his hands moving down my back and feel like throwing caution to the wind and joining the others with some action. In fact, if I am to make my screen debut with anyone, it's this sex god rubbing my body seductively, while the warm sun caresses parts of me that are never normally seen. I try to block out the sounds of fornication around me. Trust my happiest memory to be tinged with depravity. The trouble is, the sounds of their um - enjoyment, mixed with my own fantasy playing out right here and now, is starting to turn me on. Thank goodness, I must lie here and not move. I'm not sure that if I looked at Luke, I wouldn't throw myself at him with the howl of a woman possessed. So, all I do is enjoy the ride.

Finally, it's over and we hear, 'Cut.' Luke's hands leave my body and I instantly feel the loss. Sitting up, I look at him in shock and he laughs.
"That's something you don't do every day."
I giggle and look around me furtively.
"I can't believe that just happened."
We look over at the actors who are now thankfully wearing dressing gowns. The woman rushes up and thrusts my lotions and potions back at me. She pushes her clipboard towards me and says in a rush,
"Sign the release form and then you'll get your money."
Money!! This gets even better. Quickly, I sign my morality away and Luke does the same. She thrusts an envelope at each of us and then smiles wearily.
"Thanks. If you want to look the film up, it will be released in January. It's called, *Hotel Hottie*."
I daren't look at Luke, who I can tell is finding this all extremely amusing. Quickly, I grab my stuff and we both make a hasty exit.

~*~*~*~*~

Chapter 15

Finally, we locate the others. When we left the pool area we noticed that the whole hotel appeared to be deserted. Wondering where everyone was we asked at reception and were told that we had the use of the neighbouring hotel while the film crew were here.

We head across to the other hotel and I soon spy the others reclining near the magnificent pool. Jo sees us coming and I watch as a big smile breaks out across her face as she sees who walks beside me.

The others look up with similar expressions and somewhat smugly I introduce them to Luke. He nods and smiles at them and we settle down on some beds next to them.

Giggling I tell them what happened and Rachel laughs.
"It could only happen to you, Becca."
I look at her with interest.
"How did you know to come here?"
She stretches out and laughs softly.
"At breakfast. We were told the hotel was closed today and to head over here. If you hadn't slept in you would know too."

I blush as Luke grins at me. Sleep! What's that when it's at home?

Rachel smiles knowingly, and I throw her *the look* and shake my head in denial, hoping she gets the message that her perverted brain is wrong – mores the pity.

Looking around, I notice that Jenny is missing.
"Where's Jenny?"
Jo squints and looks up at the sky.
"I think she's the one in the pink lifejacket."

I follow her gaze and then do a double take because above me is a paraglider. I look at her in shock.

"You are kidding me. That can't be Jenny, she wouldn't do anything remotely dangerous like that."

Jo laughs loudly.

"Old Jenny wouldn't but new Jenny is superwoman. She came down to breakfast a new woman. After helping herself to everything on the menu she informed us she had signed up for a morning of paragliding fun."

I shake my head in astonishment as Luke looks at me questioningly. I quickly fill him in and he smiles.

"Sounds like this holiday is just what she needed. Even if she wasn't really hypnotised her mind has taken over. Good for her."

I sink back onto my towel in shock. Goodness, things are moving fast around here.

After an extremely pleasant morning, we head to a nearby café for some lunch. Jo and Rachel walk slightly in front of Luke and I and it feels so natural. Luke is good company and the best view a woman can get. He keeps us entertained with tales of life under the sea and we in turn spill the beans about what really goes on at 39,000 feet.

We are allowed to return to the hotel for the afternoon sun session and it isn't long before Jenny makes an appearance.

"Hi guys, did you miss me?"

I look up from my sunbed and do a double take.

Jenny is not alone.

She is accompanied by a beefy blonde sun god with long blond hair-surfer style and startling blue eyes. He looks like the coolest dude in the world with his man bracelets and mirror shades. She giggles as she introduces him.

"Meet Flynn. He runs the water activities centre on the beach."

I look at him with interest and notice Jenny's sparkling eyes and flushed expression. Gosh, that was fast work, I'm impressed.

Jo sits up and smiles.

"Hi, Flynn. Now, can you tell me where the real Jenny is because she appears to be missing in action?"

Jenny laughs, and grabs Flynn's hand and Rachel's eyes almost fall out of her head.

"You know, we have had the best morning ever. Flynn showed me the freedom of paragliding and this afternoon we are going on a Jet Ski safari. Do any of you fancy a ride?"

She giggles as Flynn squeezes her hand and grins at her and I look at the others in disbelief. This can't be meek and mild Jenny who is afraid of her own shadow. The transformation is astounding.

Luke looks at me and smiles.

"Are you up for a ride, Becca?"

His eyes twinkle as I try to push away the perverted thoughts of what sort of ride I want from him and I nod.

"Sure, sounds like fun."

Jo and Rachel nod in agreement and Jo jumps up. "Come on then. Show us where to go and what to do. All of this sun is bringing me out in blotches anyway."

We follow them to the beach and I look at the scary machines in front of us. I have never been Jet skiing before and if I'm honest would rather not start now. Luke must notice my nervous looks because he leans down and whispers.

"You can come with me if you like. I've done this a lot and you'll be perfectly safe."

Well, as if I'm going to turn down the opportunity to spend any amount of time with my arms wrapped around this man beside me. This is turning into the best time of my life.

Flynn gives us all lifejackets and explains how it all works. Then we watch as Jo and Rachel get on one of the machines and set of squealing towards the horizon. Luke and I are next and for the second time today I feel skin on skin with Luke, as I cling onto him for dear life.

Soon we are off and trying to catch up with the others. This is exhilarating, not the jet ski, you can keep that. It's the fact that I am face buried into Luke's back and running my hands all over his muscly body as I cling on for dear life. Never in my wildest dreams did I imagine this happening when he prowled down the tunnel to the plane.

I hear the others screams of joy and feel like joining in - although my screams are for a completely different sort of joy.

I notice with surprise that Jenny is the driver with Flynn wrapped behind her. She is laughing loudly, and I smile to myself. Good for her. I'm pleased she has finally let herself go and is having some fun. If anyone deserves it, it's her.

We must cover every inch of the bay and by the time we get back I am soaked.

As Luke lifts me off the Jet ski we stumble, and I find myself falling into the sea. He catches me and pulls me beside him, grinning. "Steady, I nearly lost you there."

I just gaze into his handsome face and my heart flutters like a romantic heroine. I feel a shiver run through my body as I look into his gorgeous blue eyes. He looks at me with that same wistful expression and I can almost taste the longing in mine. Then the spell is broken as Jo barks,

"Oh, for god's sake, can't I go anywhere without him following me?"

Looking towards the beach we see Pete waiting for us looking moody.

As we walk towards him he looks at Jo and says tersely,

"We need to talk."

She rolls her eyes irritably.

"I have nothing to say to you. Just leave me alone."

We watch as she stomps up the beach as he follows her, pleading for her to hear him out. Rachel sighs beside me.

"I wish she wasn't so stubborn. She should give the poor guy a break."

Luke looks interested and I smile sadly.

"I'll fill you in later. Come on, I think we deserve a cocktail or two after all that activity."

We follow Jo and Pete and head back to the hotel.

While Luke chats to Flynn at the bar, I fill in Rachel and Jenny about what has happened so far. They look at me with excitement and Rachel sighs. "You are so lucky. Look at him, why don't things like that happen to me?"

I look at her in surprise.

"You've found your happy ever after with Lorenzo. Surely life doesn't get any better than meeting your husband?"

Her face tightens, and she gets a sad look in her eyes. Jenny looks at me with raised eyes and I feel worried. Quietly, I whisper,

"What's the matter? You've been holding something in for the whole trip. Is everything ok with you guys?"

I watch in alarm as Rachel's eyes fill with tears. She shakes her head sadly.

"No. I don't think things are fine at all."

Jenny sits next to her and puts her arm around her shoulders.

"What's happened?"

Rachel looks so sad that I hold my breath.

"Things have changed since we got married. As you know we fell in love quickly and almost became inseparable overnight. Lorenzo was - is everything I ever dreamed of finding and I fell hard. He was always fun and good company and we were happier than anyone has a right to be. The trouble is, now we are married it's a different story. He works hard in his restaurant and I don't see him as often as I'd like. He says it's to build our future and make us secure. However, if it was just that I could understand it and support him. But it's not and now he wants me to learn Italian and take cooking lessons from his mum."

Jenny smiles sweetly.

"That's not so bad - is it? I mean, he just wants to care for you and bring you deeper into his family. Italians are all about family, so I believe."

The tears spill from Rachels eyes as she looks at us with a wretched expression.

"I wish that was all it was. He has now decided that this isn't the job he wants his wife to have. He thinks it's demeaning to him as my husband and paints him in a bad light. He should be the one to provide for his family and it looks bad that his wife is off flying around the world and not at home with him where I belong."

I share a long look with Jenny. Oh no, this doesn't sound good at all. I look at her kindly.

"Maybe he is just tired and irritable and wants you with him. He will probably come around when he is less tired."

Rachel sniffs.

"No, he told me that we are to try for a baby and start our family as soon as possible. He wants at least four children and his wife to be a stay at home mum. I must resign from my job when we return and work with him until our first child arrives."

She holds her hands up to her face and we watch the tears fall, helplessly. Jenny shakes her head at me and I look at her in disbelief. Poor Rachel.

Rachel looks up and her eyes are swimming in fresh tears.

"I can't give up the job I love, even for him. Why would he ask me to? Surely, if he loves me he would want me to be happy. Am I such a bad person that I don't want to put his needs above my own?"

I can see the guys looking at us with concern and just smile shakily at them. I pull Rachel towards me and rub her back, stroking her hair as I do so.

"It will be ok, Rachel. You must tell him how you feel. I'm sure when he sees how upset you are he will reconsider."

Jenny murmurs reassuringly.

"Becca's right. Lorenzo loves you and will want you to be happy. It doesn't mean that you won't have children in the future. Many couples work even when they do have a family and manage to lead happy lives. You must tell him how you feel because if you do as he says and give it all up you will resent him for it later on."

Rachel sniffs and looks at us sadly.

"Thanks guys. I needed to get that out into the open. Maybe I can take the rest of the trip to work it all out. I know I'm not ready to give my job up yet but I must decide is if it's worth giving up my marriage for."

I look at her in shock.

"Surely it wouldn't come down to a choice between the two? I mean, Lorenzo loves you and will want you to be happy. Maybe the two of you need this week to think about what is important to you both. I'm betting that as soon as you step foot back inside the door he will be all over you and agreeing to anything you want. This will all have been a misunderstanding and a storm in a teacup."

Jenny nods.

"Becca's right. When you get home, it will all fall neatly into place and you will wonder why you got your knickers in a twist over nothing."

Rachel smiles a watery looking smile and looks at us gratefully.

"Thanks guys, you're the best. I knew you would make me feel better."

I smile but feel the knot forming inside my chest. For some reason something is shouting a warning to me that I can't ignore. I don't think things will be ok. From the sounds of it, Rachel is in for the battle of her life when she gets home to save her marriage.

~*~*~*~*~

Chapter 16

I'm feeling quite subdued after my chat with Rachel. As I walk back to our rooms with Luke, he looks at me with concern.

"Is everything ok, Becca?"

I smile sadly.

"I'm not sure. Rachel is going through some stuff with her new husband which doesn't sound good."

I turn to look at him and smile sadly.

"It appears that relationships are complicated."

To my surprise, Luke takes my hand in his and squeezes it gently. "I think you're right. I mean, just look at my brother. It doesn't stop us wanting one of our own though. Surely, it's what life's all about. Finding that special someone to build a life with. It may not always go according to plan, but you would hope in the end you would be happy."

I look at him in shock.

Goodness, not only is he drop dead gorgeous but a nice guy to boot. Maybe I should never let this hand go and hold onto him for grim death. I wonder if I could join the submarine service or whatever it's called and be his right-hand woman? The thought of letting this hand go is choking me up inside.

We reach our rooms and he looks at me awkwardly, still holding my hand I am pleased to report.

I look into those seducing eyes and hold my breath. Something is happening, and I hope to God it's what I want it to be.

He pulls my hand towards his lips and kisses it gently.

"I've had a good time with you, Becca. When I saw you on that balcony last night something happened."

I giggle nervously.

"You found out I was a crazy person who would become one of the X Factor rejects if she ever auditioned?"

He smiles slowly.

"No, although I wouldn't fill out any applications for it if I were you."

I pretend to look hurt and he laughs softly.

"No, I realised that standing in front of me was a woman I wanted to get to know, very much indeed. Even though you looked like you'd done ten rounds in a mud wrestling contest, I saw the most beautiful woman I have ever met."

I hope they have a defibrillator handy because I think my heart just stopped. Me-beautiful? Those oysters messed with his brain and he was obviously hallucinating.

He draws me close and his mouth is inches from mine as he whispers.

"Can I kiss you, Becca?"

Resisting the urge to immediately crush his lips to mine and never let them leave, I just nod shyly.

As I close my eyes, I wait for the best moment of my life - it would appear this trip is riddled with them so far.

Before I feel the connection of lip on lip, I swear I hear music. In fact, I really do hear music. It's the sound of some sort of guitar and someone is singing in a foreign language.

Surely, it's not Luke?

I open my eyes in surprise and note the same expression in Luke's as we look around us in surprise. Standing in the hallway is some sort of Mexican band. Three guys all wearing sombreros and little matador type suits. One is playing the guitar and one is shaking maracas. The third is beating on a mini bongo drum and they are singing some sort of love song beside us.

Luke grins and keeping a firm grip on my hand, pulls me into the Love Palace, closely followed by the three Amigos.

He pulls me down onto the waterbed and whispers,

"I've been expecting them. It's all in the finer details of the package. Apparently, honeymooners get serenaded before dinner sometime during the week."

I stifle a giggle as I watch the band filling the room and singing to their heart's content. Luke grins and pulls me up.

"Would you care to dance?"

I curtsey and smile sweetly.

"Thank you for asking kind sir."

As Luke pulls me into his arms, we sway around the room to the sounds of god only knows what. If this is the song that marks the beginning of our relationship, I wouldn't know what to Google on YouTube for our first dance wedding song. It doesn't matter though because it could be the Birdy song for all I care. I am in Luke's arms in a honeymoon suite being serenaded by a love trio. The fact that they interrupted the next best moment of my life doesn't matter. I am just loving feeling his hard body pushed against mine as we spin around his decadent room. I shift even closer - shamelessly and allow myself to dream that this is our honeymoon and we have a whole life together to look forward to.

Then the miracle happens. Luke pulls back and looks deeply into my eyes. As if in slow motion I watch his lips lower towards mine and my heart races. This is it! It's happening! Then I feel his soft lips claim mine in a toe-curling, life-changing moment of deepest joy. I sink into his mouth and never want to leave. It feels as if I'm home.

We kiss for ages, really, we do. The band left ages ago, but we didn't even acknowledge them. Luke and I are locked at the lips and never letting go. I forget that I need air to breathe and just take my oxygen from him instead. Who knew kissing would be so good? If I did nothing else this week, I would be happy. However, as they say, all good things come to an end and he pulls apart and looks at me with a sexy gleam in his eyes.

"So, as first kisses go, that would be considered quite memorable - wouldn't it?"

I laugh a little self-consciously.

"Yes, it would be difficult to top that one."

He grins and tilts my face to his.

"I'm always up for a challenge. Let's see if I can make this one even better."

Then all praise to Aphrodite, we go at it again.

Reluctantly, I leave Luke and head back to my trashed room in a daze. I am in love. I don't care that it has been five minutes, I know I am. Lust doesn't come into it, ok well maybe a little, ok maybe a lot. The things is, I really do think I'm in love. Luke is everything I want in a man and strangely my heart seemed to know that the minute I saw him walk onto the plane. What I'm finding it hard to get my head around, is that he appears to like me too.

Taking extra care, I get ready for the evening ahead. Marcus will be shocked when he sees me with Luke. I'm not sure where he's been today but I can't wait to see the look on his face.

I dress in a clinging black dress that means business. I need Luke to see me as somebody that he must never let go, because submarine or not, he is going to feature in my future. I just know it.

It must be an hour later that I hear a knock on the door. As I open it, my heart flips as I see a washed and scrubbed up Luke filling my doorway. He smiles, and I watch his eyes brim with lust as he takes in the sight of me. I'm sure my eyes must mirror his because he takes one step towards me and takes up where we left off an hour ago. Who cares that my lipstick must now be all over his face? I kiss him back like a woman possessed and shift closer just to feel that body against mine.

Pulling back, he whispers huskily.

"Sorry, Becca. You make the gentleman in me leave the building. I can't help myself when I look at you, you're gorgeous."

I stop myself laughing hysterically. Me - gorgeous! I love him now, it's official.

He pulls back, ruefully.

"We had better join the others before they send out a search party."

Then he grins.

"You may want to re-do your lipstick first though."

Grinning, I pull him into my room.

"Ok, I won't be a minute."

The trouble is, as soon as we get inside he pulls me towards him and we're at it again. Now I have a man in my designer room and I'm out of control. I have become sex mad woman overnight and all of my usual standards have been chucked over the balcony. I am no prude but entertaining a man in my room is unheard of. I'm just not like that. It's funny how morality goes out the window when natural urges take over.

Once again, we reluctantly pull apart. Moving across to the mirror I laugh at the red smear on my face. Luke joins me with an equally smeared face and we laugh at our reflections.

Handing him a wet wipe, we clear ourselves up. After a further application of lipstick - to my lips, not his, we head down to meet the others. We walk there hand in hand and very much an item, for a few more days, anyway.

~*~*~*~

Chapter 17

Marcus's face is a picture as we emerge from the lift and join the rest of them. He bounds towards us and looks at us both incredulously.

"Since when did this happen? I've only been gone for a few hours and missed all the action."

I laugh and flick him a mischievous smile.

He shakes his head and then addresses the group.

"Come on, I've booked us a boat trip around the bay. Elvis and I have arranged for a night of pure joy on the ocean waves. There will be lots of Mexican food, tequila, and shameless conga dancing as we sail around the bay."

I look over and note Rachel's sad expression and my heart lurches. Poor Rachel. She is in hell over there, so I pull Luke over to join her. I look at her sympathetically and smile.

"Come on, Rachel. Lots of tequila for you tonight and I expect you to show us all how to conga like a pro."

Jo races over and looks angry.

"Great, now a whole night confined on a boat with Hugh Hefner's replacement over there. He won't leave me alone, despite the fact I've told him I'm not interested in his explanations."

Rachel rolls her eyes and looks at her sternly.

"Let it go. Perhaps you should just let him try to explain. It's obvious he's feeling bad about the whole thing. Maybe it will take locking you both in a cabin together to make you see sense."

Jo shrugs and looks down. Despite her hard exterior I know she is hurting, and that is why she can't forgive him so easily.

We are interrupted as Jenny bounds up, Flynn in tow.

"I can't wait to set sail. I have discovered a new love of water and this will be awesome."

Jo looks up and smiles.

"You're right, Jenny. Let's just go and have some fun."

The boat is anchored off a jetty not far from the hotel. It appears that we aren't the only ones to set sail. I look with trepidation at the sheer amount of people heading onto what is quite a small boat. Then I look at Luke with a worried expression and whisper, "Do you think it's safe?"

He grins, and grabs hold of my hand, squeezing it gently.

"I'll protect you. I know quite a lot about evacuating a ship should the need arise."

Why do images of the film Titanic spring to my mind? I shiver inside. The fact that Luke's hand is holding mine so tightly is doing strange things to me inside.

We follow the others on board and I note the flashing lights and the scrubbed deck of a large cabin. Tables are placed around the edge of a large dance floor and the noise is off the scale.

Music thumps out from large speakers and to say the whole thing looks tacky would be an understatement.

We find an empty table and place our drinks orders with Barry and Pete. I sit between Luke and Jo and look at the other people around us. It appears that this is the Party boat because every other person it seems is intent on having a good time. Inebriated guys knock back shots of tequila, with shorts as chasers. Girls scream and totter around the dance floor as if they are possessed by an uncool demon. They also appear to be somewhat worse for wear and the boat hasn't even set sail yet.

I laugh as I see Marcus dressed up like some sort of tourist in a Hawaiian shirt with a feather boa draped around his neck. He is being pirouetted around by Elvis the concierge who is certainly taking his duties seriously in showing his guests a good time.

Luke nudges me and I look over at Jenny and Flynn who appear to be recreating the scene from Dirty Dancing. They are pressed together and gyrating to the tune of, Esposito and I grin as I see how happy she is.

As Barry and Pete head back with our drinks the boat suddenly lurches and moves away. This is it, no going back. The only thing keeping me from totally freaking out is the thought that if I die, I would die happy with Luke beside me for eternity. I have always believed that when you die you go to heaven with the others that die with you. Sort of like passport control. Loved ones who have gone before, meet you on the other side in Heaven Arrivals. If you've been bad you are pulled aside by security and sent downstairs. The trouble is, only my childhood cat would be waiting for me, unless you count my ancestors who I don't really know. Even in death, I would be forced to live alone.

Luke nudges me out of my contemplation.

"Do you fancy a dance, Becca?"

Quickly, I push my seat back hoping it isn't obvious that I can't wait to be in his arms. Grinning, he pulls me onto the dance floor and my wish is granted. As I feel his strong arms circling my waist I feel as if I'm in heaven already. Would it be in bad taste to press myself against him like Jenny is having no trouble doing to Flynn? I've always been quite reserved and old habits die hard. Instead, I just allow myself to be led around the dance floor by my officer and a gentleman.

After a while, I feel Luke pull me closer and I shift so there is no air between our bodies. The swell of the waves and the effects of the tequila work their magic and I close my eyes and savour the feeling. Luke leans down and presses his cheek close to mine and I feel his breath on my face. His strong hands rub my lower back and I am grateful for the loud music because I'm so ready to start groaning again. The music starts to fade in the background as my senses go on full alert. It's just the two of us in our own little section of paradise and I try to stop myself from singing Fernando again. I don't know why I always sing that stupid song when I feel happy or sad. I've grown up with it and it has sort of become my theme tune through life. I wish I could have thought of a better one.

Despite the fact that the songs are fast and loud, and the crowd is wild, Luke and I dance as if the song is slow and seductive. All around us, people are doing the sort of Dad dancing that should be banned in public places. Women jump up and down, shaking their heads and all of their assets, as they roll around the dance floor as the waves take them. Guys are doing some sort of weird robotic numbers while they openly stare at the women's chests. Marcus appears to be doing some sort of 'Oops Upside Your Head' dance on the floor with Elvis between his legs and some guy dressed like a sailor behind him. Jo and Rachel are dancing demurely on the side watching Jenny and Flynn sex dance in front of them.

Luke and I just move. That's all - we just move. There is no art to our movements and we are just hug dancing. The sort that shuts everyone else out and is just an excuse to have our hands all over each other legitimately in public.

I close my eyes and sink into his chest and his arms tighten around me. How did I get so lucky?

For the most part, the evening is a lot of fun. I enjoy dancing with my friends but not half as much as enjoy dancing with Luke. The trouble is, as the alcohol takes hold, things start to go downhill really quickly.

By now I have downed more tequila shots than I think is humanly safe for my body and am feeling pleasantly happy. Luke is similarly affected, and we look around us with the smug looks of those who have it all. Jenny and Flynn are now openly snogging in the corner and Jo stands up and pulls Rachel with her.

"Come on Rach, all of these loved-up couples are making me want to launch myself over the edge of the boat. Let's just dance and block this love fest out."

Rachel grins as she follows her, and I snuggle deeper into Luke's lap, which for the last thirty minutes I have sat on with his arms wrapped around me. Pete and Barry have taken up residence at the bar to avoid Jo and I watch my friends hit the dance floor, with as much abandon as two uptight girls with a lot on their mind can do. I even think they are the only sober ones on board because I have noticed they are both on the soft drinks tonight.

Luke starts kissing my neck which deliciously distracts me as we start making out at the table. Gosh, I feel like a teenager; I am loving this trip!

Suddenly, I hear shouting and look up in alarm. It takes me a moment before I see what appears to be an almighty fight breaking out on the dance floor. I hear screaming as all hell breaks loose.

We jump up and I watch in horror as Luke dives into the fray, pulling people out of the way and dodging punches as he goes.

He emerges from the riot pulling Pete away from some guy with blood dripping from his nose. Jo is shouting angrily, and Rachel is pulling her away.

I look around and notice that Jenny and Flynn seem unaffected and carry on kissing in the corner - really!

Rachel drags Jo over and I note the angry tears streaming down her face as Luke bundles Pete outside on the deck. I shake my head in confusion as Jo starts sobbing next to me.

"What happened, Jo?"

She sobs

"Some guy tried it on with me on the dance floor and Pete saw him. I pushed the guy away, but he pulled me back and the next thing I knew, Pete waded in and punched him. The guy's friends joined in and started hitting Pete, so I tried to pull them off. Then Luke waded in and sorted them out and Barry helped."

She looks up, the tears running down her face.

"Do you think he's ok? He took quite a few hits and there was a lot of blood?"

Rachel looks visibly shaken and says in a low voice.

"I'm sure he's fine. It's probably best that he went outside. We don't want any more trouble."

Grabbing her hand, I squeeze it reassuringly.

"It will be fine. It's what happens when alcohol flows so freely."

Just then, Marcus rushes up with a concerned looking Elvis. He holds his hand to his heart and looks at us with wide, dramatic eyes.

"Oh my god, girlies, that was so hot. I've come over all damsel in distress. What I wouldn't give for guys to fight over me like that. If I were you, Jo, I would be outside on that deck pressed up against my hero. That was so hot."

Rachel grins and shakes her head as Jo rolls her eyes and hisses angrily.

"Oh, shut up, Marcus. None of that was hot and sexy. If you must know I hate violence and fighting and that has just put me off him even more. I'm glad he's outside so I don't have to see his face because he's the last person I want to see at this moment."

Marcus shakes his head and rolls his eyes.

"Keep telling yourself that, Jo. I saw the look in your eyes when he was in the thick of it. You can deny it all you like but nobody believes you. You are punishing yourself more than Pete by keeping up this angry charade. For god's sake just go and make up and do us all a favour. This is starting to get old."

He flounces off and Rachel looks at me and grins.

Jo just looks annoyed and shrugs.

"He's so irritating sometimes. He thinks he knows it all, well he knows nothing. I have every reason to be angry with Pete and it's not just because of Margaret."

She flounces off in the other direction and Rachel looks at me with a dumbstruck expression. "What do you think she means?"

Shaking my head, I look at Jo's retreating figure thoughtfully.

"I think there's something she's not telling us. Nobody holds this much anger for so long against somebody who they are obviously mad about, without a very good reason. I wonder what it is?"

Rachel shrugs and looks concerned.

"We'll get it out of her by the end of the trip. Just you wait and see."

~*~*~*~

Chapter 18

Luckily, we make it back to shore with no further trouble. We head back to the hotel a little subdued after the evening's events. Pete looks as if he's been in a boxing ring and I can see the bruises forming on his face. Jo ignores him and looks angry and withdrawn and as soon as we get back to the hotel, she stomps off to her room. Pete and Barry also head off and Rachel sighs beside me.

"I think I'll call it a night. All of this excitement is draining. I'll see you at breakfast, guys."

We nod and say our goodbyes as Marcus links arms with Elvis.

"Come on, I think they're still serving at Los Romanticos. There's a drag act on tonight that I've heard is panty melting amazing. Come on Elvis, let's salvage the evening somehow."

They head off squealing like a couple of girls as they race towards the bar on the strip. Jenny gazes at Flynn and then says softly.

"Sorry guys. Flynn and I are heading back too. See you in the morning."

My mouth falls open as I watch his arm go around her shoulders and they head towards the hotel. I can't believe what I'm seeing. Jenny, apparently, has no reservations about taking a strange man to her room. Lucky cow.

Luke looks at me thoughtfully.

"So, what shall we do now?"

As I look into his gorgeous eyes my heart does a little sexy dance for him. I can picture exactly what I want to be doing next and its right in front of me. The trouble is, I'm a good girl and have been for the last thirty years. I can't appear to let that go, despite the fantasy staring at me with hunger in his eyes. I shake my head sadly.

"I don't know, really. Maybe we should call it a night too."

He looks at me with a touch of regret in his eyes and just smiles sweetly.

"Of course. You must be tired after such an exhausting day. Let me escort you to your room. Before you object, I promise it's not out of my way. I mean, I can't have you wandering the hotel corridors on your own without protection, what sort of officer would I be then?"

I laugh softly, feeling relieved that he isn't annoyed with me. I bet he's cursing his luck to be stuck with the frigid one and on his honeymoon at that.

He holds my hand as we walk back to the hotel. It feels nice and safe and I hate myself for not being some sort of wanton hussy that would be all over him in a heartbeat. We could have so much fun. However, I'm conscious that in a few days he will be gone from my life back to the submarine, leaving me to my spinsterhood once again.

I try to tell myself all the way back to my room that I should live a little. Let go of my morals and throw caution to the wind. This could be the memory that sustains me in my lonely future. I will look back on it fondly as being the best week of my life. I should be more like Jenny and embrace the moment and give in to my wanton desires. The trouble is, I can't. It's not me and I can't change who I am. I want the fairy-tale not the x-rated kindle book version. The trouble is, at this moment in time I hate myself for it.

We reach our rooms and stare at each other, both unwilling to let go of the other's hand. Luke stares into my eyes and then pulls me towards him, whispering, "Thank you for an amazing day and an eventful night. I've had a good time."

I smile shakily.

"Yes, me too. It's been good."

He touches his lips to mine and I savour the feeling of them. I could kiss this man all night and for the rest of the week before coming up for air.

He pulls back and smiles gently.

"Listen, if you don't have anything planned tomorrow, would you like to come on a trip with me?"

I look at him in surprise.

"What is it?"

He grins.

"Apparently, the honeymooners are due to visit a romantic Island for a picnic. They will be taken there by speedboat and left to spend the day in solitude. I wasn't going to go but think it may be fun, but only if you're with me."

He looks unsure and I feel the light enter my heart again.

I say softly.

"I would love to come. What time do we leave?"

"10am. If you like you could join me for my romantic bedroom breakfast and then we could go after that."

I smile at him happily.

"It's a date. I'll knock on your door at 9."

Once again, we indulge in a little lip action before we reluctantly head to our respective rooms.

The morning comes, and I wake up with a happy heart. I get to spend all day with Luke away from civilisation and nobody around to judge me. I wonder what we will talk about? I wonder if we will move this thing on we've started? I wonder if we will discover that we really hate each other. It's possible after just one hour locked away on a deserted Island with only the coconuts and sea turtles for company. But most of all, I wonder how much longer I can keep from falling head over heels for the man who has bulldozed his way into my heart so quickly.

By now my room is back to well-ordered perfection. I couldn't rest until every towel was folded and straightened on the rails. Each item of clothing was colour coordinated in the wardrobe and my shoes lined up in order of size and colour. My toiletries are once again facing the right way in order of use and the wet wipes have graced every surface, removing any bacteria or other people's DNA. I take a deep breath and look around at my orderly life with satisfaction. Finally, my head is as tidy as my room and I can breathe again.

As soon as I knock on the door, it opens, and my breath catches as I behold the object of my desires. He grins at me with that lethal smile and it's the hardest thing to stop myself launching myself on him with a frustrated spinster style howl. Instead, I smile my nearly perfected mysterious woman smile and follow him inside.

Today we breakfast on the balcony and I sigh as I see the bay laid out before us like a sparkling blue lagoon. The sun is hot already and I feel the excitement growing at the promise of a day marooned with Luke on a deserted Island.

We feast on pastries and fruit with the odd yoghurt thrown in and then Luke looks at his watch.

He turns to me the excitement shining in his eyes.

"Come on. We're due to leave in ten minutes. I wonder what it will be like?"

I smile happily.

"Probably amazing like everything else here."

He nods. "Yes, this place is pretty amazing."

I feel his eyes burning into mine as he says it, looking at me with a heated gaze. As I feel the hot flush exploding inside me, I wonder if the air-conditioning has broken.

Shaking myself out of yet another hot, crazy fantasy, I look around at the remnants of the breakfast.

"Do you think we should bundle the rest of this up and take it with us? I mean, you never know, we may not like the picnic."

Luke grins and his eyes flash with amusement

"Yeah, sure. I'll grab a bag. You never know, we might be glad of this if we are stranded."

He winks and goes off to grab a bag while I wrap up the leftovers to take with us. Then I contemplate the mini bar.

"Should we raid the bar as well? It would be awful if we ran of something to drink."

Luke laughs and opens the door with a flourish.

"Hm, let me see. Gin, vodka, wine - what's your fancy?"

I laugh and peer in, selecting two bottles of chilled water instead. He raises his eyes and I pretend to look at him with a stern expression.

"You shouldn't drink alcohol in the sun. It's extremely dehydrating and could mess with your mind."

He snorts.

"That would explain a lot."

Nudging him, I take great delight watching him fall over and he looks at me with a challenge in his eyes.

"You'll pay for that."

As I dodge to safety on the opposite side of the huge water bed, I really hope that I do pay for it. In fact, I don't mind paying for it for the rest of the holiday. I laugh and quip.

"You'll have to catch me first."

He lunges for me and I make a dash for the other side of the room. He's not a trained military man for nothing though and soon takes me down. He sits astride me, pinning my arms above my head and grins.

"You're now my prisoner and will be escorted to the Prison Island. There, you will have to exist on vodka and yoghurt for at least five hours, in extreme temperatures that will mess with your mind."

I snort and then look at him with embarrassment. Whoever invented snorting when they invented humans was having a bad day at work. How is that considered a good thing in any situation?

I just giggle and then my heart flutters as Luke leans down and kisses me softly. Willing myself not to groan and add to my bodies betrayal after the snorting incident, I just allow myself to enjoy the only thing I really want this week - Luke's lips on mine.

~*~*~*~*~

Chapter 19

Ok, whoever chose this Island as a paradise escape for couples in love, was having a laugh.

First, we endured a reckless speed boat dash across the bay where I feared for my life. Then, we were abandoned on an uninhabited Island with nothing but a box - and I mean cardboard box- of food and drink.

There are no sun loungers to recline on, no pool to take refreshing dips in and no bar to swim up to for a thirst quenching cocktail.

They haven't even raked the sand like they do on the hotel's private beach. There are also twigs, and leaves mixed in with the odd bit of sea fodder, littering the beach area.

Luke looks around him and whistles as we watch the retreating boat speed off back to civilisation.

"Well, this is unexpected."

I shake my head, looking around me with dismay.

"Do you think they brought us to the right beach? I mean, call me mad if you like, but I'm sure if this had been in the brochure it wouldn't have sold the experience. It's a mess."

Luke looks worried.

"I'm sorry, Becca. I thought we would have a lovely day in a place not dissimilar to the one they use on Love Island. This is more like a survival programme."

Laughing, I roll my eyes.

"Lead on, Tarzan. We may have to fashion a shelter out of a few palm trees and build a fire using our sunglasses to catch the sun's rays."

Luke grins and dumps the picnic box on the floor.

"It may not be so bad. I expect what we're really here for is just around that corner, like an oasis in the desert. I'll race you to the beach front bar."

He sets off and I chase him in hot pursuit. Of course, he's right. There must be five-star excellence just around the headland.

Ok, we have now run around this Island in ten minutes and every bit of it is the same as the first. This place is seriously in need of development. There isn't even a hammock to erect between the twin palm trees that are swaying in the gentle breeze. Luke looks worried.

"I'm sorry, Becca. This isn't what I hoped it would be."

I shrug. "It's fine. I'm sure we just need to place our towels on the sand and sunbathe while pretending we are in luxury. The time will pass by in a flash."

Shaking out my towel, I lay it neatly on the sand and then grab my suntan lotion. I try not to ogle Luke as he rips off his t-shirt and flops down beside me. That body will melt all of my principles by the end of the day if he continues to wave it in front of my face.

Carefully, I strip down to my bikini and start applying the lotion. Luke watches, his head propped up by his hand as he lies beside me.

"Do you want me to do your back?"

I shrug nonchalantly while trying to stem the raging lust within me as I imagine his handling of my near naked body.

"Sure, thanks."

He jumps up and grabs the bottle from my hand with rather a lot of enthusiasm and says gently.

"Lie down so I get good coverage."

Trembling inside, I do as he says and allow myself to enjoy the administrations of my fantasy love god. Gosh if

Marcus could see me now he would be insanely jealous. How I wish I could take a selfie and send it to him.

Focusing hard on not groaning, I try to start planning my Christmas list in my mind to offset the pleasure my body is receiving. After quite a while Luke finishes and immediately I feel the loss of his touch. Sitting up, I almost drool as I say matter-of-factly.

"Here, let me return the favour."

He chucks me the lotion and I allow my hands to roam freely all over his body. I take my time to enjoy the sight of those muscles rippling under my shaking fingers as I fantasise about what could happen if I allowed it. Luke groans and I feel a small victory. Huh, now we are even in the groaning stakes. He can no longer tease me about my lack of control. Leaning down, I whisper,

"Did you just groan, Luke?"

He laughs softly.

"Sorry, Becca. You've got to remember I live at sea. I don't get to feel a woman's hands on my body very much, so I apologise for my lack of self-control."

I feel the fire burning in my face at his words. Either that or the sun is out of control and inflicting sunburn on me as we speak.

I say softly as I rub.

"It must be hard being at sea all the time. You must get quite close to your fellow submarinist members."

Luke chuckles.

"Another professional term. Do you write for the Thesaurus in your spare time?"

I giggle and carry on rubbing as he laughs.

"I try not to get close to any other members on board. It's not really my thing."

Pushing him, I roll over onto my towel and prop myself up in a similar pose to his, so we are facing each other.

"What's it like living under the sea like Neptune? Do you see treasure and fallen galleons? Are there mermaids and ferocious sea creatures to contend with? Is Atlantis real and have you been there? Have you ever seen another submarine and visited?"

Luke leans over and silences me with a kiss. Suddenly, I couldn't care a fig for life under the sea. Life on a dirty Island is becoming just that as I kiss Luke back with everything I've got.

As Luke and I make out on dirty Island all of my fantasies are coming true. I'm almost hoping that the boat never comes back because then we would have to live here forever like they did in that film, The Blue Lagoon. As Luke's hands start their wandering my anxiety makes another unwelcome appearance. I must stiffen because he pulls back and whispers.

"Is everything ok, Becca?"

I look at him with troubled eyes.

"I'm sorry Luke but what if there is somebody around? What if they have cameras here to check we're ok and not in danger from fearsome sea turtles and poisonous spiders? I'm sure I saw a flash of light in the distance which could be from someone's binoculars as they watch our every move. I'm sorry, but even on a desert Island, all I can think of is the sand in my knickers and how long it will take to get it all out. Not to mention the fact that my suntan lotion has acted like a sand magnet and I'm now covered in grit. I suppose I could wash it off in the sea but what if there are jellyfish and conga eels? I'm just one anxiety filled mess and you are probably regretting ever inviting me."

Luke sits up and laughs loudly.

"No problem, Becca. I'll admit it's not very comfortable. How about we brave the sea and I'll protect you? I mean, I was trained by a merman once in the art of sea survival, so you will be perfectly safe."

I giggle as he pulls me up from the sand.

"Come on, I'll race you."

We race towards the sea, leaving my anxieties behind on the sand. Who cares if I die at sea? At least I will have lived a little first.

Frolicking in the sea with Luke is every bit as amazing as rolling around with him on the sand. My inhibitions desert me, and we play fight, kiss, swim and talk while being bathed in the crystal-clear water. Luke is such good company and the conversation never dries up. We talk about everything and by the time my skin resembles a prune I feel as if I have known him all my life.

We retreat back to the beach for our picnic.

As we share out the rations, I look around with interest.

"I wonder how many other couples have visited this beach. I wonder what they did to pass the time?"

Luke grins and I giggle nervously.

"Do you really think they... you know... um..." I lower my voice to a whisper, "Do *IT* on here?"

Luke smiles sexily.

"Most definitely. They are on honeymoon after all. My bet is they're at it all the time at every presented opportunity."

I blush, and look interested in my papaya. Luke pours me some of the champagne that was provided with the picnic and passes me a handful of strawberries.

"We may as well enjoy the rest of what they've provided though."

As I take the glass from his hand, I feel like such a fool. Opportunities don't ever come around like this and here I am letting my insecurities getting in the way of what could be the most romantic experience of my life. Luke must think I'm a weirdo. Then he says softly.

"Look at me, Becca."

I raise my eyes to his and see the soft sexy look he is shooting me, and my heart starts pounding in my chest. He says softly.

"You must know that I like you a lot. You are everything I never thought I would meet one day and everything I hoped to. When I took this holiday, it wasn't to meet and fall in love. I was just here for the break and a bit of luxury before I return to my metal home. When I met you, things changed. I watched you on the plane and couldn't get you out of my mind. When I knew you were staying at the same hotel, I emailed them from the transit bus to ask for you to be put in the room next to me. Even then, there was something compelling me to get to know you and find out if the woman who captivated me was what I thought."

I look at him in astonishment.

"You really did that?"

He nods and looks at me with a soft expression.

"I don't have long before I leave and didn't want to waste any time. I don't want this to be the end but the beginning of something special. When we return home, I want to see you again and keep in touch. I can wait for you to be comfortable with me before we take it further, because if I have to, I will wait a lifetime. I think you're worth the wait because I have been waiting for you all my life."

Ignoring the warning siren going off in my head that he is a typical sailor spinning a line, I smile and say softly.

"I like you too, Luke. I'm probably just afraid that this will all end and am protecting my heart from the inevitable shattering it's about to receive. More than anything, I want to let go and be the sort of person I have been encouraging Jenny to be, but I can't. I don't want you to think that I'm the sort of woman who does this with any willing sailor that passes her door. It matters what you think of me."

Luke pulls me close and touches his lips to mine, then says softly.

"Trust me, Becca. I'm not the rogue you think I am. Contrary to public opinion, I don't have a girl in every port and there is nobody else on the horizon. You are everything I want and I will wait as long as it takes."

Then he kisses me so sweetly and the little doubtful voice in my mind is replaced by my braver self, shouting, "For god's sake, idiot. Grab him and never let go. Do whatever it takes because this is the best opportunity of your life."

So, I give into my desires and push the doubt away. Who cares if it all goes wrong? The memory of this will keep me warm as I reminisce with my potted plant about the day I lived on the edge.

~*~*~*~*~

Chapter 20

I never thought my walk of shame would be in a speedboat. As soon as the driver came to collect us I didn't miss the knowing smirk on his face or the amusement in his eyes. I can't blame him because I must look a total sex hussy mess. My hair is all over the place and filled with sand and parts of beach matter. The sand has stuck to my skin and my flushed appearance has nothing to do with the suntan that I'm sure to have after rolling around naked on the sand for the last two hours.

I feel different. Now I feel like a woman who has changed in a matter of hours. I feel fulfilled and in love. What just happened with Luke was everything I thought it would be and much more. Any doubts I had are firmly buried in the sand we disturbed because he has made me feel like the most gorgeous woman on earth.

He puts his arm around me as we speed back to civilisation and whispers, "No regrets, Becca?"

Snuggling into him, I sigh with contentment.

"No, none. What about you?"

He squeezes me tighter.

"Are you seriously asking that? I've wanted to do that since you read out that stupid message on the plane, that I wrote, incidentally. It was my idea of a joke to my brother that backfired quite spectacularly."

Giggling, I lay my head on his shoulder.

"Well, I'm glad it happened. Their loss is our gain, although I never expected to meet my dream man on his honeymoon."

Luke laughs and kisses the top of my head.

"Yes, it's an interesting story. We will keep our kids entertained with it for years."

A warm feeling spreads through me at his words. Our kids! I hope the overexposure to the sun hasn't affected his brain because I want to believe every word he says. This man is my future I have never been surer of anything in my life.

Once we get back to civilisation I am surprised to see a large shape on the horizon. Luke looks at me with excitement. "If I'm not mistaken, that's one of ours."

I look at him in surprise.

"What do you mean, *one of ours*?"

As we both contemplate the extremely large warship that appears to be invading Acapulco Bay, Luke grins.

"It must be one of our Naval ships on exercise. I'll head over later and see if I can find anyone I know."

I laugh. "They won't let you on there, you're now officially a tourist."

Luke grins. "They will. I am an officer of her Majesties armed forces after all. They are my family and it would be rude not to visit."

He takes my hand and pulls me after him towards the hotel.

I now feel like a new woman. Luke and I returned to our rooms and showered and changed. He has headed off to the warship and left me to find my friends with the promise of meeting up when he returns. I can't ignore the warm glow that surrounds me as I think about the day I've had. I actually think this has been the best day of my life. How can it not be? I fell in love with my soul mate. Life doesn't get any better than this.

I spy Jo lazing by the pool and glide over in a self-satisfied haze. Arranging my towel and products neatly beside her she looks up and grins.

"Where have you been because wherever it was I want a ticket? You look mightily pleased with yourself."

Smiling smugly, I settle down beside her.

"Let's just say this is turning out to be the best trip ever. I am now officially in love with the man of my dreams and may never return home in case the bubble bursts."

Jo smiles happily.

"Lucky you. You deserve it. He seems really nice, and it's about time you found some happiness."

I note the catch in her voice and look at her with a worried expression.

"How about you? Have you forgiven Pete yet? If it's any of my business, I really think it was just a silly mistake. He obviously idolises you."

She sighs heavily and looks so sad it takes my breath away.

"I wish I could, Becca. It's not just about Margaret anymore. If it was, I think I would have forgiven him already."

Gently I say, "What is it then?"

She shakes her head and looks at me sadly.

"Listen. Don't tell the others but I think I may be pregnant."

Well, I wasn't expecting that and look at her in shock.

"Oh, my goodness, Jo, are you sure?"

She nods. "I'm late and one thing about me is I'm never late in any aspect of my life. Ordinarily, I would be over the moon. I know that Pete and I aren't married but we live together and it's just a formality, really."

I smile softly.

"So, what is the problem then?"

Her eyes fill with tears and she looks out to the Bay with a lost expression.

"It's this Margaret thing. What if I can't trust him? You know what the pilots are like. They have many a temptation thrown in their path as soon as they put on that damn sexy uniform. What if he has met someone else and is stringing me along? You know as well as I do that it happens all the time. Even if they're married, they stray, and I don't want to bring a child into an uncertain future."

I think about her words carefully. I know she is wrong about Pete. Yes, he's a good-looking guy who could take his pick. I also know that he is crazy stupid in love with my stubborn friend and his behaviour this trip has just cemented my opinion. I turn to her and smile.

"Why don't you talk to him? Tell him about your suspicions and lay it all out in the open. At least give him the chance to explain and you will know in his eyes if he is telling the truth. His reaction to your news will speak volumes and then you will have your answer."

She looks thoughtful as we are interrupted by Rachel and Jenny heading our way.

Immediately, I sense Rachel's disapproval as they draw near and the look she throws me is one of utter horror. I sit up and watch them approach and look at Rachel with questions in my eyes. She shakes her head and nods pointedly towards Jenny and I wonder what has happened now.

As they spread out their belongings, Jo looks at Jenny and says loudly.

"Good God, Jenny, did something happen? You look as if you've had an accident."

I look at Jenny and notice a large bandage type thing pressed to her upper right arm. She winces and smiles happily through the pain.

"Oh, this. It's not what you think."

Rachel looks at her with irritation and says somewhat sharply.

"Tell them what you've done, Jenny."

Jenny grins and slowly peels off the bandage and Jo and I gasp in disbelief. Among the red, sore mess on Jenny's arm appears to be a tattoo - quite a large one, of the letter F surrounded by a wave.

Jo looks at me in horror and exclaims.

"Jenny, you stupid idiot. That had better be a transfer because if its permanent the sun must have gone to your head and rendered you an idiot."

Jenny just laughs happily.

"Impressive, isn't it? Flynn and I got these done this morning. He has a J and I have an F."

Rachel looks at her with irritation.

"And what happens when you return home with this permanent reminder of your trip? How will you explain the F on your arm? F for fling, or F for fucking mad."

Jenny looks unconcerned.

"It won't matter because as soon as I get home I'm quitting my job and heading straight back here to run the water sports business with Flynn."

There is silence. Stone cold disbelieving, what the hell just happened, life-changing moment silence, as we all look at Jenny in total and utter disbelief.

She laughs at our expressions and sinks back onto her sunbed with a sigh of contentment.

"I've decided that life is for living and seizing the moment. I'll no longer be concerned about the mundane and have decided to embrace my wild adventurous side that has been buried deep within me for so long. Flynn has brought that out of me and we have discovered that we are two sides of the same coin. He has begged me to stay, and I didn't need asking twice. This is my home now and I couldn't be happier."

For once in her life, Jo is lost for words and Rachel shakes her head in disbelief. Then I watch in shock as her eyes fill up and she looks at Jenny with admiration.

"Good for you, Jenny."

Jo looks astonished.

"Don't encourage her, Rachel. She should be told that this is a very dangerous plan. Flynn could be some sort of mass murderer who lures innocent, unsuspecting, vulnerable girls to his lair. He knows that Jenny is a lost soul and plans on stripping her of her inheritance to feed his obvious drug habit. Mark my words this will end in disaster."

Jenny looks at Jo with an angry glare.
"Just shut up, Jo. You know nothing. Flynn is the most open, honest man, I have ever met. He is a free spirit of nature and came here from Australia two years ago. He said that when I return we will live here for a few more months until we have saved enough money to move on to the next country. He intends on travelling the world and wants to take me with him. So what if it's reckless? I don't care because I have been sensible for far too long. This is my time to shine and I can't wait to take this journey with the first man I have ever loved."

She huffs and pulls on her sunglasses and lies back on her sunbed. Jo shakes her head and Rachel sighs sadly.

"Good for you, Jenny. You're right, life is for living and you should do whatever makes you happy. You have taught me that. I wish I was as brave as you."

I look at her with a worried expression and say softly.

"Are you ok, Rachel?"

She smiles weakly.

"I will be, Becca. I just need to sort things out at home first."

~*~*~*~*~

Chapter 21

As I get ready for the evening, I hum a little tune in the shower. I can't believe how happy I feel. Today has changed my life and what happened at dirty beach will keep me warm on many a cold night. Even if Luke and I fizzle out, nothing can take away the memory of an extremely hot day at the beach.

On the dot of 7, there is knock on the door and I feel that delicious fluttering feeling inside. I wonder if things will have changed between us? Taking a deep breath, I open the door and smile at the extremely sexy man filling my view. Luke grins and my heart beats faster as his eyes almost strip me bare with longing. In just one small move he is before me and takes me in his arms, whispering, "Evening sexy girl. I missed you today."

Trying to look cool and sexy, I fail miserably as a huge grin breaks out across my face.

"Hi, yourself. How was the boat? They let you leave then."

He raises his eyes. "Boat!" Shaking his head, he smiles. "The correct term is Ship and you would do well to remember that when you are mingling with the Navy elite at the Captain's cocktail party tomorrow night."

Just for a moment, I don't think I register his words and look at him with a puzzled expression.

"I'm sorry, what did you just say?"

He laughs and pulls me closer, whispering,

"We've all been invited to the usual cocktail party that the ships have when they dock at a new port. The Captain said your crew would be most welcome as it's normally just local government officials and dignitaries. He said his men would thank him forever for injecting a bit of life into the proceedings."

I know my face must be betraying the thoughts that are all running through my head at once.

This is a one hundred percent dreams come true, is this really happening? wait until I tell my friends moment.

Squealing, I fling my arms around him, shouting,

"Oh. My. God! I can't wait. Thank you, Luke, you're amazing."

Laughing, he rolls his eyes.

"Just remember I'll be there to make sure those rampant sailors keep their distance from you. After their lonely nights at sea, they will be hot on the prowl and the sight of a group of gorgeous girls will bring out the caveman in them."

Shivering with delicious anticipation of a night surrounding by her Majesties finest, I grab his hand.

"Come on, let's tell the others. You'll be their superhero after this."

I drag him to the party room with not a moment to lose.

Marcus actually screams - yes screams - with excitement when I tell the packed crew room what Luke has arranged. The excitement is off the scale as every last person takes in the news of the treat awaiting us. Pete looks amazed and smiles at Luke.

"Thanks, mate. I would love to see around a Navy Ship. Are you sure they don't mind though? Is there any security clearance we need to go through first?"

Shaking his head, Luke smiles.

"No, usually these things are pretty boring. They invite the local officials in return for docking at their port. Just lots of small talk while sipping wine and nibbling on canapes. It sounds a lot better than it really is."

I don't think one person in the room agrees with him. Oh no, this doesn't sound mundane at all. This sounds like the gods love us and have made all our dreams come true. I can't wait until tomorrow, it will be the best night of my life - ever!

As nights in Acapulco go, tonight is fairly tame. We all head off to eat and I enjoy holding Luke's hand and feeling the envious gazes of any female within looking distance. Luke is the hottest guy I have ever met and for the next few days he's all mine. I'm trying not to let the thought of what will happen when our time is up affect me. I will just enjoy the moment. Jenny and Flynn are as into each other as usual and I wonder if she is ready to give everything up to return here and be with him. I expect if Luke asked me I would. Maybe it's true and love does hit you like a lightning bolt, making you do rash, crazy things that have no place in a rational person's mind.

Catching sight of Jo pointedly ignoring Pete, I worry about her. The pained expression on her face and the hurt in her eyes reveals there's a lot going on in her mind at the moment. Pete wears the same expression and I hope for both their sakes they work it out. They may have to if Jo is correct and expecting a mini version of the two of them to arrive in just under nine months' time.

After a calm, enjoyable evening, Luke walks me back to my room. My heart starts thumping as we head upstairs, and I wonder what happens now. This is now really awkward. Do we continue where we carried off on the beach, or do we continue as before and just go our separate ways to bed?

I'm not sure what I think about either and worry that whatever decision I make will be the wrong one.

As soon as reach our rooms, Luke looks at me and smiles.

"Thanks for a great evening."

I smile, and he pulls me close and whispers.

"I hope this doesn't make you feel uncomfortable, but I don't want to let you go. Will you spend tonight with me in my brothel room? We don't have to do anything, just stare at ourselves in the mirror if you like. I just don't want to waste a minute of the time we have left without you being by my side."

I look at him shyly and nod.

"I would like that, Luke."

As he pushes his key card in the door, my heart starts beating like a drum at a rock concert. Am I really going to do this?"

Once inside the Love Palace, I look at his red bed with horror. All over the bed are rose petals looking like a hurricane has blasted through a rose garden. Luke laughs as he sees my expression.

"Mad isn't it? I'm not sure why they think this is romantic. It's just irritating having to remove them from the bed before you can go to sleep."

He starts to brush them away and I feel my OCD kicking in as I start to remove them carefully. I'm happy to say that once I delve deeper into the floral extravaganza, I find some lovely little chocolate hearts mingling with the horticulture. Throwing one to Luke, I roll my eyes with joy and groan as the sweet chocolate hits my taste buds.

"Hm, this is worth the clean-up operation. You didn't say you got chocolate. I would have been here much sooner if I knew about these."

Luke grins and nods towards the bathroom.

"They usually put a few in there as well. First one to find them wins."

Before he even finishes the challenge, I'm on it. We both race for the bathroom and I push him out of the way to be the first one to reach the sweet reward. As I push open the door, I'm amazed to see candles burning brightly everywhere. There is a bucket of ice holding tightly onto a bottle of champagne, next to a bowl of strawberries by the bath. Luke grins as I clap my hands with girly excitement.

"I love your honeymoon, Luke. I take it all back, Mexicans know the way to a girl's heart. Look at this place, it's every girl's dream."

As I look at him I do a double take. He is looking at me with such a loaded - lust filled look, that I swear my legs almost give way.

Suddenly, any doubts in my mind are thrown quickly over the edge of the balcony. There is not a woman alive who could resist this. As Luke moves towards me I meet him halfway and then there is no stopping us. Hot nights in Mexico don't come much hotter than this and now there is no holding me back.

~*~*~*~*~

Chapter 22

Waking up the next morning, I wonder why I am moving. It feels as if I'm on a boat cast out to sea. I'm aware that I'm not alone. As I feel the pressure of a warm body pressed close to mine, the memory of the night before comes flooding back.

I freeze as the morning shame hits me. What did I just do? All of my morals and code of conduct disintegrated as soon as Luke tore off his t-shirt. The sight of that body heading towards me shattered my principles in a heartbeat. I quickly close my eyes as he stirs beside me. What must he think? He must think I'm some sort of hussy who does this sort of thing all the time with random guys I pick up abroad. The worse thing is, I'm sure I have rose petals stuck to every part of my body. I also have bed hair that has no business being seen by a dream god like Luke.

He snuggles into me further and I lie like a stiff board next to him. What on earth will I say to him when we actually have to speak to each other? Will he look at me and regret the alcohol intake that has clouded his mind into believing I'm a supermodel and not some ageing spinster from Crawley who spends her days talking to a potted plant?

The bed continues to rock me on my walk of shame - again! How many more times will I take this walk this week? Will I ever feel comfortable with the decisions my harlot of a mind makes for me when I'm under the influence of lust and alcohol?

I brave a look and wince at the sight that greets me in the mirror above. I'm entwined with a sex god on a bed of roses; one of which appears to be stuck to the side of my face. I can see another one on Luke's back and feel my fingers itching to pull it off. However, as I take in the sight of his muscled body hugging mine, my inner devil looks at me with admiration and pride. Way to go, Becca. Memories don't come sweeter than this and who cares about morality anyway? Enjoy every second because life is for living. If I remain alone for the rest of my life, nothing can take away what happened last night.

Luke stirs beside me and whispers sleepily.

"Morning, gorgeous. Did you sleep well?"

Shamelessly, I snuggle beside him and move even closer.

"Yes, thank you. Despite the fact the bed moved and was the strangest feeling ever I slept really well."

He pulls me even closer, if that's possible and says huskily, "Honeymoons are the best, aren't they?"

Grinning to myself, I nod slowly.

"Well, this one certainly is. That's for sure."

After the night of my life, we eat the honeymoon breakfast as if we've been starved of food for a week. As we sit on the balcony looking over the bay Luke says with interest.

"What did Marcus arrange for today again?"

I smile and roll my eyes.

"Apparently, Elvis's cousin runs boat trips out to see the famous Cliff Divers of Mexico. He is taking us all on a trip to see them from the bay. There will be food and drink on board and it should be a relaxing trip while watching brave men jump to their possible deaths for our entertainment."

Luke grins.

"Sounds good to me. Although, I would be more than happy just to spend the day rubbing suntan lotion on your back and hearing you groan some more."

He laughs as I look at him with embarrassment.

"You just caught a muscle, that's all."

He laughs. "I seemed to catch a lot of them last night if I remember."

Giggling, I throw a banana at him. "Says you. You added a few groans of your own to join mine if I remember rightly. In fact, it was a groanathon marathon."

Luke laughs. "Groanathon. I've been at sea too long. I have missed this recent evolution of the English language."

Shaking my head, I grin and once again thank the gods for giving me such a hot groaning partner. Who wouldn't groan at the sight of this man in their field of vision? Groans must follow him wherever he goes.

As we get ready to leave, I wonder what the day will bring. One thing's for sure, boats are going to play a large part in it.

With our beach gear in tow, Luke and I meet the others in reception. There are quite a lot of us going on this trip and I think the whole crew is here. There is a lot of excited chatter as we wait for the fun to commence.

Rachel comes over and grins. "This will be a busman's holiday for you, Luke."

He laughs. "Almost. Though this time I will be out in the open and not submerged at thousands of feet below civilisation."

Rachel looks interested. "It must be a strange way to earn a living."

He nods. "It is. It's only when I have leave that I remember there's a world out here. Most of the time I love my job but the realities of what it's costing me is starting to weigh on my mind."

He looks at me with that same wistful expression and something catches in my heart. He looks lost and unsure and I instantly want to pull him closer and reassure him that everything will be ok. We share a small smile which changes into a loud laugh when Marcus pitches up with Elvis in tow. They look every inch the nautical sailors, or should I say naughty. Marcus has a Captain's hat perched on his head at a jaunty angle. He is also wearing a t-shirt with— *'Master Bates'* emblazoned across it with the image of its namesake in full Technicolour glory. Luke laughs beside me as Jo says with horror,

"You can't wear that, Marcus, it's obscene."

He grins. "No, Jo, it's just your mind that's obscene. This is a much-loved cartoon hero from my youth and I won't hear a word said against it."

Rachel grins as Marcus claps his hands.

"Right then. Elvis's cousin is Captain Elviras. He is waiting for us by the jetty. We need approximately five hundred pesos each for this trip, payable on embarkation. There will be a small picnic provided by the hotel in lieu of us missing lunch. We will be heading over to watch the famous Cliff Divers and afterwards will sail back in plenty of time to get ready for cocktails aboard HMS excitement. Now, does anyone have any questions?"

He looks around and smiles happily.

"Come on then, follow me to the Love Boat."

Luke and I walk with Rachel and Jo, as Jenny and Flynn bring up the rear. We chat generally but I notice the strain in Rachel's eyes. Maybe I should make a point of getting her alone on this trip. She needs somebody to confide in, I can tell. This might be just the opportunity to help out my friend.

Captain Elviras speaks no English and just smiles at everyone. He looks at us with what can only be described as a mass murderer, *'I am going to drown you all,'* glint in his eyes. As we look at his boat, I feel a little dubious. It appears big enough for all of us but what happens if we need to abandon it? I can only see a few inflatable rings hanging on the side.

I turn to Luke and whisper, "As ships go, it's not very big, is it?"

He rolls his eyes. "No, Becca, this is a boat, not a ship."

I frown and look annoyed.

"Oh, make up your mind. Boat or ship, what is the correct term?"

Luke laughs and grabs my hand, squeezing it gently.

"According to the Royal Naval Institute, a boat, generally speaking, is small enough to be carried aboard a larger vessel. A vessel large enough to carry a smaller one is a ship. The only boat this one could carry is a toy one. Later on, you will see the difference between the two."

Once again, the excitement fizzes through me at his words. A real-life navy ship party with my very own officer escort. I am certainly living the dream this week.

Once we are all onboard, we set sail or whatever it is these boat ships do. Everyone makes themselves comfortable by sprawling on the deck and catching some rays. Marcus and Elvis hand out drinks from a cooler and I watch as the boys try their hand at a spot of fishing. I position myself next to Rachel and Jo, with Jenny on the other side and we lie back in contentment.

Rachel sighs beside me.

"This is what makes the endless tedious hours of drinks, meal and duty-free worth it. If only every week could be like this."

Jenny laughs softly.

"You're right. I suppose when I move out here it will be for me. I mean, I'll get to work on the beach every day and wake up to the beautiful sunshine. Thankfully, I will be leaving the cold, grey winters behind."

Jo says somewhat sharply.

"I hope you know what you're doing, Jenny. Maybe you should wait for a few weeks before handing in your notice. I don't know, maybe book a holiday out here first and see how you get on."

Rachel nods. "Jo's right. It may help your decision. Take it from someone who knows. When the first flush of love dies down there is a cold hard reality waiting to take its place. You may regret your decision and have to come home to an uncertain future."

Jenny looks at Rachel thoughtfully.

"You're talking about yourself, aren't you?"

Rachel looks at us sadly.

"I think I am. Lorenzo and I rushed into marriage without really getting to know each other properly first. Lust clouded our view and when it faded, I realised he wasn't the man I fell in love with. I still love him, but we want different things. He fell in love with an independent woman who loves to travel and take on life's experiences. The woman he wants is someone who stays by his side and provides him with a family. He wants me to learn Italian and convert to the Catholic faith. What scares me the most is I obviously don't love him enough to do it."

Jo reaches out and grasps her hand.

"Rachel, the most important thing is to do what makes you happy. If you're miserable, then he will be too.

Lorenzo loves the woman you are and not this mother substitute he has in his mind. Maybe you should both just sit down and discuss your feelings. You may find you're making a big deal out of nothing. Once he knows how you feel he will come round."

Rachel smiles and then says somewhat harshly.

"Right back at you, Jo. Maybe you should follow your own advice with Pete. I mean, look at him over there. He pretends to be interested in fishing, but he can't take his eyes off you. I can see the hurt in them from here. What's stopping you from following your own advice and sorting it out?"

Jo just looks at her with a hard expression.

"It's different."

Jenny rolls her eyes.

"Not really, Jo. Whatever made him say Margaret's name shouldn't be the cause of you splitting up. I'm sure it was just a mistake. My mum used to call me by the cat's name all the time."

We all laugh, and Jo rolls her eyes. "Well, we haven't got a cat called Margaret or a dog or a goldfish or a bloody pot plant. Therefore, your theory falls apart under the briefest scrutiny. No, whoever Margaret is, she is the person responsible for breaking up a once happy couple."

Silence descends, and we lie back, her words ringing in our ears. There will be no arguing with her when she's in this mood. Jo sees things in black or white. There is no grey area, and she makes no excuses. Maybe that's why she's finding it so hard to forgive Pete.

As I think about it, I enjoy the gentle rocking motion of the boat as the sun beats down onto my bare skin. This is actually a very pleasant trip. I have heard of the famous Cliff Divers. They stun the gathered crowds with their deaf defying leaps from a great height into the rock-laced waters below. This should be interesting.

~*~*~*~*~

Chapter 23

"I think I'm going to die."

I run my tongue over my lips, trying to get some moisture in them. Jo's words echo my own thoughts as the boat lurches from side to side. My whole body is moving in different directions to other parts of me and my head is spinning. I feel the bile in my throat and my head is so heavy that I think it has been super-glued to the deck. I can't open my eyes because the sun is too bright and burns through my glasses. There is silence all around.

All I can hear are the groans of my fellow sailors as everyone lies flat on the deck. The rolling and pitching of the boat is doing strange things to my mind and body and I actually think I am going to die.

There is not one member of this boat that isn't similarly affected. Even Luke is clinging to the side rail and leaning over the side of the boat. Barry is sitting with his head in his hands, groaning. I see Pete out of the corner of my eye crawling across the deck towards Jo, who is groaning loudly as she lies face down.

Marcus looks green as he sits with his back against the side of the boat and every other person is clinging to something to try to stop from falling over.

Only Captain Elviras and Elvis appear unaffected and look at us with worried expressions.

Suddenly, the Captain cries out in Spanish - I think and Elvis translates.

"We're here, everyone. Look, the cliff divers are diving for your pleasure."

Jo groans loudly.

"The only one I'm interested in seeing throw himself off that cliff is now invading my personal space. Clear off Pete, I blame you for all of this."

Pete says in a strangled voice.

"If we die on this boat, I just want you to know that I love you, Jo. There is no Margaret and never has been. Not even a relative or old classmate. I swear on my life it was nothing, just a weird reaction to the passionate moment."

Jo growls. "Shut up with your passionate moments. You can keep them to yourself in future. Just leave me alone. I'm about to die and I don't want yours to be the last voice I hear."

I hear somebody throwing up over the side of the boat and try to blank it out. If I hear the sound of retching I am liable to join them. This is a disaster.

Soon the groans turn to moans, interspersed with heaving and retching. I actually think Jo is right. We are all going to die.

After the worst couple of hours of my life, Captain Elviras takes us safely back to shore. We leave the boat on very shaky legs, followed by the Captains' very worried expression. I almost feel sorry for him as he looks so upset. I can't even raise a brave, farewell smile because my world is still spinning and I'm not sure if my legs work on their own anymore. I don't think any of us even saw the famous divers, so it was a complete waste of time.

Somehow, we manage to drag ourselves back to the hotel and our respective rooms. The thought of getting on another boat in just a few short hours is not a happy one, despite the man candy on board. Luke came back to my room because he couldn't face lying on a moving bed while feeling the effects of our boat trip. Instead, we just lie on my massive bed which is the size of a small island and fall into a sickness induced slumber.

It's amazing what a few hours rest on solid ground will do. We are soon scrubbed up and loaded with excitement at the thought of the evening to come.

Luke looks good enough to eat in a pair of smart black trousers and a white shirt. He has scrubbed up well and I almost wish we could stay in tonight.

I have tried my best and am wearing the favoured blue dress and high heels. I've curled my hair and applied my make up as best as I can, given that my head is still a little shaky from earlier. Either that, or the sight of Luke sitting on my bed looking like Christian Grey, with those sexy smouldering lust-filled eyes completely directed at me.

He smiles and says gruffly.

"You had better stick close to me tonight. One look at you and there will be a stampede."

His words make me giggle stupidly and I shake my head.

"Don't be silly, nobody will give me a second look."

I hope against hope itself that I'm wrong, as I contemplate the image of a ship full of lust crazy sailors stampeding towards me. Now that's an image that will keep me warm for the rest of my life.

For the first time I can ever remember the crew is silent as we contemplate the immense beast before us. HMS Richmond is the name of the absolutely huge Naval ship currently gracing the shores of Acapulco. There is a long gangplank bridging the gap between the shore, at the foot of which are standing two sailors dressed in their sexy white uniform. We look at them in total awe and for the first time since I have known him, even Marcus is quiet. Luke takes hold of my hand and winks.

"Relax, Becca. It's not so special."

I shake my head in total disagreement. No, this is one hundred and twenty billion percent special in my eyes. This is the moment of a lifetime.

Like Noah's animals, we head on board, two by two. Luke and I lead the way and I swallow nervously. We reach the top of the gangplank and Luke salutes the two officers stationed at the top. He states who we are, and the extremely hot sailor consults his clipboard and ticks us off with a flourish of his pen. Then he salutes as we walk on past.

I look around me in sheer disbelief. This just can't be happening. All around me is regulation grey paint. The whole ship looks complicated and fearsome as I gaze up at the elements of war all around us. Large solid doors guard their secrets against prying eyes and I feel so small and insignificant.

We make our way to a large deck area which is obviously the scene of the soiree tonight. All around are white-clad sailors mingling with the locals who look every bit as intimidated as I do. Luke guides us over to a man chatting in a small group and waits until the man looks our way. I watch as he salutes him and then proceeds to introduce us to what I now know is the Captain.

I shake his hand and worry that I should curtsey. What's the protocol for one of these things? Unlike Captain Birdseye, this man is elegant and poised. His clipped British accent rings out in pure authoritative style as he welcomes us all onboard.

Then we fade out of his sight as he greets much more distinguished guests than we are.

Luke pulls me over to a group of officers and one of them smiles and winks at him.

"You made it then."

Luke grins.

"As promised."

He turns to us and smiles.

"Meet Tom. He's promised to arrange you a guided tour of the ship if you want."

I almost shake with excitement. Wow, this is like a dream come true.

We are organised into groups of four. Luke, me, Jo and Rachel.

Jenny, Flynn, Pete, and Barry are in a group of their own and Marcus, Elvis, Caitlyn, and Michelle make up another. The rest of our crew are divided into groups and I swallow hard as what can only be described as a Tom Cruise lookalike smiles around at us.

"I'm Mark and I'll be your guide this evening. Have any of you ever been on a Naval ship before?"

Rachel grins. "I went on the Cutty Sark once on a school trip. I'm betting things have changed since then."

Mark looks at her and his eyes twinkle. "Just a little. Anyone else?"

Luke just grins and Mark laughs.

"I'm sure Luke can answer any questions you have as well. He may travel under the sea instead of on top, but the principles are the same."

As he sets off, we follow him, exchanging looks of pure excitement as we go.

As we follow Mark and Luke around the ship I shudder inside. All this grey is seriously creeping me out. It's so boring. Why didn't they consult the Farrow and Ball catalogue? It would be much more stylish than gunmetal grey on every surface. Maybe I should suggest it to the

Captain over a canape and glass of fizz later. I may even offer my Interior design skills and help design a new fleet of ships 'a, la, Laura Ashley.' They would all thank me for enriching their lives.

Mark explains the different uses of the rooms, or should I say cabins, that we come across. He even shows us the Captain's quarters and I'm sorry but green flowers went out in the seventies. I've heard of budget cuts but surely they could run to a few new curtains here and there.

The most exciting part was when we got to sit in the chairs on the bridge. We posed for many a photograph while pretending to save the world.

Moving from the top we venture lower down. I look at the huge steel doors with an almost panic attack. Luke whispers, "These doors have to be heavy and thick. Each sailor has a section to man and if there is any danger, they have to secure the door to save the ship."

I look at him in surprise.

"What, if pirates came on board?"

Luke laughs.

"No, the biggest fear is fire or water. These doors are designed to keep both out. Even if it means trapping your fellow sailors behind them, your first priority is to protect the majority."

I shiver at the thought of what they may have to do.

As we descend even further, the temperature increases. It gets extremely hot and I wonder if health and safety know about this. Mark notices our flushed faces and smiles.

"We're getting nearer the engines down here. This is what powers the ship and the conditions are extreme. It doesn't help when you're in a hot country either."

I hang onto Luke as we progress. I don't miss the curious stares from the sailors that work here. Most are dressed differently to the officers on the top deck and I whisper to Luke.

"What's the differences in the uniforms?"

He whispers. "These are the Ratings. They work under the officers and all have a specific job to do."

As we meander through the ship, I am in awe of the scale of the operation. Mark shows us where they all work and some of the cabins that they sleep in. There is hardly any room for them to sleep and the conditions are cramped. Even the officer's cabins are small, and I think of my huge room back at the hotel. Why would anyone enjoy living here?

I notice that Rachel chatters to Mark constantly. She asks him lots of questions and he appears very pleased to answer. Jo, however, is uncharacteristically quiet beside me. I nudge her and whisper,

"Are you ok, Jo?"

She nods. "I'm fine. I think that boat trip earlier affected me more than most. I can't seem to get myself back to normal."

I link arms with her and smile.

"Lean on me if you like."

Looking around, I whisper, "What do you think of this? It's amazing isn't it?"

She smiles. "I've never seen anything like it in my life. Hats off to them, I couldn't exist without a nice bath followed by Emmerdale every evening. This would send me crazy being cooped up in here."

I nod in agreement. "Have you noticed there are lots of women? They're not stupid, are they? I mean, adrift on the ocean waves with a ship full of hot guys. It may be worth putting up with the cramped conditions if it means getting up close and cramped with some of these."

We start to giggle like schoolgirls and Luke rolls his eyes.

"Come on, we'll head back, and you can grab some food and drinks."

By the time we re-join the party I almost feel as if I could go on Mastermind with my newfound knowledge. One thing I have learned is that it's most definitely not a sailor's life for me.

~*~*~*~*~

Chapter 24

It's such a relief to get outside in the fresh air. We stand huddled together and look around with interest. Luke takes my hand and smiles. "So, what do you think?"

I look at him with excited eyes.

"I think this is a once in a lifetime experience that I will never forget, thanks to you."

He laughs. "You're easily pleased."

Rachel grins.

"I'm with Becca on this one. There aren't many people who get to do things like this. I never thought I would."

Mark smiles at her and a little dart of worry pierces my heart. Surely Rachel will remember she is a married woman, even with all of this temptation on board. I watch as she laughs at something he says and catch Jo's eye. She just shrugs and looks over to Pete who is chatting with another group of people. I watch her eyes narrow as she sees Pete laughing with a glamorous woman. Barry heads over and she pounces on him immediately.

"Who's that woman shamelessly flirting with Pete?"

Barry looks over and then shrugs nonchalantly.

"I think she's the British governor's secretary. I believe her name is Margaret."

Jo's face is a picture as we all dissolve into hysterics. Barry snorts.

"You should see your face, Jo. No, I think her name's Verity. She was just happy to chat with some other British people. Apparently, it's quite lonely living as an ex-pat."

Jo just glares at the chatting couple and if looks could kill, they would both be in a watery grave by now.

I see Marcus holding court among a bunch of officers and smile at the excitement on his face. He is loving every minute of this and I'm sure we will hear of nothing else for months. At least he can tick another uniform off his Village People list.

Jenny and Flynn are chatting with another group and I feel happy that we are all having such a lovely civilised time.

As Mark guides Rachel over to another group nearby I whisper to Luke.

"I'm not sure we should leave Rachel with all this temptation. She's vulnerable at the moment and liable to do something she may regret."

He looks thoughtful. "Maybe she needs to cut loose for the evening to remember what's important in her life. Sometimes the grass looks greener until you start running through it. Then you look back and see that grass is better than the one you're in now. She may realise her husband is all she wants, and this will just cement her decision."

Jo interrupts. "Or it may just show her what she's been missing out on. Mark my words, it will end in disaster. Becca's right, we need to keep our eye on Rachel tonight and save her from herself."

I watch as her eyes flick back over towards Pete and see the tears welling in her eyes. I sigh irritably. There's another one I need to keep my eye on. This is getting ridiculous.

As the evening wears on we have the time of our life. Soft music plays in the warm balmy breeze and the motion of the waves rocking the boat gives off a sense of peace and calm. All around is the soft rumble of conversation and lots of laughter and clinking of glasses. Luke and I mingle with many officers and I enjoy listening to their nautical banter and comparisons about life on and below the ocean waves.

I notice that Rachel and Mark have struck up quite the friendship and worry about my friend's decisions in life.

It must be one hour later that I notice Jo looking a little green. I head over and whisper,

"Are you ok, Jo?"

She looks at me with a miserable expression and looks towards Pete who is still laughing with his glamorous companion. "I think he's just given me my answer, don't you? I knew he wasn't to be trusted."

Shaking my head, I smile at her gently.

"He's just being friendly. I've seen the way his eyes have followed you all evening. He has had one eye on you the whole time. You really should give him a break and make up. It's obvious you're both hurting."

She just smiles sadly and once again looks a little odd. Feeling worried, I whisper,

"Shall I get you a glass of water? It's quite hot out here and you look in need of it."

She nods gratefully. "Yes, you're right. It's ok though, I'll just head over and grab one from the waiter."

She walks away unsteadily and then before I can even move to follow I watch almost in slow motion as she falls gracefully to the deck.

I scream, "Jo!" and all eyes turn to her. As I rush over I am joined by half the ship's crew as they surround my friend, who has passed out quite spectacularly in full view of everyone. Pushing my way through the gathering crowd I see an officer kneeling beside her. He looks up and says seriously,

"Back away everyone. She's fainted. She may have hit her head, so we can't be too careful."

By now Rachel and Jenny have pushed their way through accompanied by a distraught looking Pete. He crouches down beside her and takes her hand in his.

"Jo, it's Pete, please say something. It's ok sweetheart, I'm here."

The officer looks at him. "Do you know if she has taken anything, or on any medication that I should know about?"

Pete shakes his head in confusion.

"What are you talking about? Of course not. She's just fainted, probably due to the heat and the motion of the boat."

The officer looks at him sternly. "That may be the case, but we have to establish the facts first before moving her. I may need to call an ambulance and they will need to know everything."

I look at Rachel and Jenny and see the same worry etched on their faces as on mine. I wonder if I should say anything about her suspected condition.

She appears to be still out cold, and the officer looks worried. As I make my decision, so apparently do my friends because simultaneously we all blurt out, "She may be pregnant."

Pete looks up in total shock. "Since when?"

The officer looks even more concerned and calls out to some nearby officers. "She needs to get inside out of the heat."

We look on in shock as Jo is lifted carefully into the arms of a burly sailor and carried off to safety. Pete races after them looking as if he may also faint at any moment.

The three of us follow, accompanied by Luke, Flynn, and Mark.

I feel extremely worried that I have blurted out Jo's secret in front of her Majesties Navy and Pete. This may not go down well at all.

~*~*~*~*~

Chapter 25

Jo is taken to the ship's medical room and we wait in the officer's mess. Pete stayed with her and the rest of us look at each other with worried expressions.

Rachel shakes her head. "I hope we haven't blurted something out we shouldn't have."

Jenny nods miserably. "She's going to be so mad at us. I thought I was the only one who knew because she told me not to tell anyone."

I nod in agreement. "Me too."

Rachel agrees. "Me too."

Luke laughs softly.

"It would appear the only one she didn't tell was the possible father to be."

Rachel looks worried.

"Poor Pete. That must have come as quite a shock.

We all nod and fall silent as we think about the sparks that about to fly.

Mark looks at us reassuringly. "She'll be fine. It happens all the time. People aren't used to the motion onboard a ship and what with the temperature, I'm just surprised she was the only one. That's all it will be, and you will laugh about it tomorrow."

Rachel smiles at him. "Yes, you're probably right. You must be regretting inviting such a group of landlubbers on board."

I watch as he throws her *that look* - you know the look of the interested, and my anxiety levels reach code red. Then he says. "Why don't you all come back tomorrow night? We have an officer's party here in the mess and you would certainly make it more fun than the usual ones we have."

Rachel looks at him, her eyes shining. "Are you serious? That would be amazing."

Jenny and Flynn nod in agreement and I look at Luke with trepidation. Shrugging, he just smiles. "Thanks, I'm sure everyone would love it. What time does it all kick off?"

"Come around 9 pm. It's not much, just a few drinks and some music. We're here for a few days so we may as well have some fun."

As he says it he turns to Rachel, and she smiles at him with a smile that has no business being directed by a married woman. This is not looking good for Lorenzo.

It must be half an hour later that the ship's doctor comes in and updates us on Jo's condition. He smiles at our worried faces.

"Your friend will be fine. She just fainted as we thought and didn't hurt anything on the way down. I'm not sure about the ship though."

We laugh politely but my anxiety is overpowering my mind as to what is going on in there now. Jenny says hesitantly.

"Is… um… Pete still with her?"

The doctor smiles.

"Yes, I believe they are having quite some conversation in there. I thought I'd best leave them to it. It would appear they have some matters to sort out."

Luke takes my hand and says, "Come on, let's give them some privacy. I think there may still be a few glasses of champagne left upstairs."

We follow him back to the party but I'm sure I'm not the only one who dreads what will happen when Jo catches up with us.

The rest of the night passes uneventfully. I just enjoy spending time with Luke on board this impressive vessel and try to burn the memories into my mind for posterity. If this all ends in a few days' time I will need to call on them to get me through life. How can anything ever top meeting this dream guy and experiencing the ultimate trip of a lifetime? I try to ignore the little voice inside me shouting that I'm heading for a very big fall from a great height when this bubble bursts.

Shortly before we leave, Jo and Pete re-surface from the sick bay. My heart lifts as I see them walking hand in hand with extremely happy smiles on their faces. They head over and the three of us look at Jo guiltily.

I say somewhat nervously, "Are you ok, Jo? I'm so sorry we blurted out your... um... condition."

She surprises me by just laughing happily.

"Think nothing of it. It had to come out sometime and what better way than that. I'm not going to lie, the thought of all those hot sailors coming to my rescue is a dream come true."

Pete frowns and Jo giggles and kisses him on the cheek, saying, "But there was nobody I would rather wake up to than this gorgeous man of mine."

Rachel looks confused. "That bump on your head must have either knocked some sense into you or erased your memory. What did we miss?"

Jo laughs.

"When I came round and saw Pete gazing at me with so much love, I knew that he was mine. I may have been annoyed with him but that doesn't matter anymore. It's his face that I want to see every day for the rest of my life because despite what has happened, I love him. We talked, and I told him of my worries and insecurities."

Pete nods and looks at her fondly.

"She should have said something earlier. As if I want anyone else when all I ever want is here holding my hand. The thought that we may become three is the best news I have ever had."

He kisses her lightly on the lips and then pulls away and drops to one knee before us all. I gasp, as I reach for Luke's hand. Oh my God, this is so happening right before my eyes and those of the Queen's men.

We all stand watching what we know is going to happen, in complete silence. Pete looks at Jo adoringly and says softly.

"I love you, Jo. You are my girl and always have been. You are the one I want to spend the rest of my life with. The one I want to love and protect and devote my life to making you happy. There is no room left in my heart for anyone else because you fill it so completely. Please, will you marry me Jo, and make me the happiest man alive?"

There is silence as the whole ship watches the spectacle. All around us is a sea of white uniforms and speechless guests. Everyone holds their breath as a huge smile breaks out over Jo's face accompanied by a whole lot of tears. Nodding furiously, she shouts loudly, "Yes, I'll marry you. Of course, I will."

Then they are hugging and kissing as loud cheers break out all around the ship. The music starts up again and we all surge towards the couple to congratulate them. As I hug my friend, I feel the tears spilling down my cheeks. "Congratulations, Jo. I know you will both have a long and happy life together."

I watch as Rachel squeezes her tightly and note the tears in her eyes. Jenny shrieks and dances up and down on the spot as Pete shakes hands with everyone that he can.

I look at Luke and he smiles at me and my heart melts. What I wouldn't give to end up with him. How lucky would I be if that ever happened? The trouble is, the moment of truth is fast approaching and it's scaring the hell out of me. How will I bear to say goodbye to the man who has captured my heart?

~*~*~*~*~

Chapter 26

Luke and I are fairly subdued as we head back to the Love Palace. I'm not sure why but seeing his life up close and personal brought it all home a bit. When this week is over, it will be hard to say goodbye. We have only known each other for a few days but I feel as if I have known him a lifetime. They say this happens in books and films, but I never thought it would happen to me. It's going to be hard going back to Malcolm and the realities of my lonely life. Maybe we will become pen pals and just reminisce about the one thing we have in common - Mexico. Then the letters will become less frequent and the whole glorious dream will fizzle out.

Once we are back to our rooms Luke looks at me with a lost expression. Pulling me towards him, he whispers,

"Please stay with me tonight, Becca. I'm just conscious that we only have a few more days and tonight has brought it home. I'm due to return to work soon and may be away for some time."

He looks at me nervously.

"I can't ask you to wait for me, that would be selfish. A beautiful woman like you could have her pick of the guys who must hang around you all of the time."

Gosh, Luke doesn't know me at all. Tequila certainly messes with the head. He smiles anxiously.

"When we get home, can I still see you whenever I can?"

He smiles and his eyes twinkle as I hold my breath. Something is happening here and my heart is racing as I swallow hard. He cups my face in his hands and the look he throws me would melt an iceberg.

"I suppose what I'm trying to say is, will you be my girlfriend, Becca? I've wanted to ask you that all week but thought you would think I'm some sort of madman for rushing in so quickly. But I know deep down that you are the one for me."

Tears spring to my eyes as we stand in the hallway of the Emporio and I nod slowly. "Well, I knew as soon as you walked onboard the aircraft, so I win."

Luke laughs and then without any further delay, kisses me so passionately I think I will burst. This is what I've been waiting for all my life - him. The trouble is, I am destined to be like Elizabeth Swan on Pirates of the Caribbean and wait for my Will Turner to return every ten years. It will be worth the wait though. I know in my heart that I can cope with a long-distance relationship as long as Luke is at the end of it.

Waking up in the Love Palace the next morning feels different. Now I am officially allowed to be in Luke's bed because we are - a couple! Maybe we will become like those super cool couples who finish each other's sentences and wear matching sweatshirts. Ok, maybe that's not so cool, but the thought of introducing my boyfriend to my family is the best feeling I've ever had. Gosh, Kieran is nothing like Luke, my sister will be so jealous. I'll be able to show him off at family parties and everyone will envy me. He will only have eyes for me, though and I will glance around with smug satisfaction at the jealous, envious, looks thrown my way. Oh, I hope there's a school reunion. Imagine their faces when I rock up with Luke on my arm. Matthew Billingshurst will seem like Quasimodo next to Luke.

As I plot out the tour of my past to showcase my new boyfriend, the man himself stirs beside me. Quickly, I glance in the mirror above the bed, checking that I look like a sex siren and not my usual mess. His arm reaches out and pulls me close and he whispers, "Morning sexy. I like waking up with you."

Trying not to giggle stupidly; I mean, sexy? Me? I just smile in my new mysterious way.

"Did you sleep well?"

He nuzzles my neck and pure happiness consumes me. "Hm, did you?"

"I did actually. I never thought sleeping on water would be so restful. I may have to invest in one of these for myself when I get home."

Luke looks into my eyes and my heart almost stops. Sexy morning Luke is totally irresistible. His sleepy eyes look sexy and the designer stubble on his chin makes me want him to rub it all over my body like one giant exfoliator. He smiles.

"When we get home, I still have a week before I'm due back. If you have any days off and fancy it, would you like to come home with me and meet my parents?"

Oh. My. God! Meet the parents! This is serious. I smile at him with excitement.

"Of course, I would love to meet your family. Won't they be surprised though? I mean, in less than a week you've gone on a honeymoon and returned with a stranger. It may well send them over the edge after what happened with your brother."

Luke laughs. "They will love you on sight. In fact, don't be surprised if they start talking about wedding bells before they've even made you a cup of tea. I told you, they are desperate for me to settle down and leave the Navy."

I look at him thoughtfully.

"And what about you? What do you want?"

He pulls me close and growls, "I think you know the answer to that. What I want is right here and I am never letting you go."

As we cement our newly formed relationship alliance, I think I am the happiest I've ever been in my life.

We spend the rest of the day sunbathing. It would appear that most of us are now worn out and need to rest and recharge before our wild night out with her Majesties' Navy. Luke is sprawled out next to me on his sunbed with his headphones on and there is not a more heavenly sight. Rachel lies next to me and I decide to have a chat with her in advance of tonight's temptations. Nodding over to her I say, "Do you fancy a cocktail?"

Grinning, she grabs her sarong and we head off to the bar.

As we sit waiting, she sighs.

"This is all so perfect, Becca. Out here we have no ties or obligations. There is no daily routine to follow and no demands on our time. We can be whoever we want to be and there are no consequences. I couldn't give this up and live tied to a pram or a kitchen sink. It's just not me."

I agree with her, it's not. But the trouble is, she has made her marital bed, and she does have responsibilities and the consequences of her actions waiting for her back at home. I smile reassuringly.

"You know, all of this isn't real, Rachel. It's just a bubble we live in for a few days before real life comes to claim us back. Trips like this happen so few and far between. Take it from one who knows, it's lonely living on your own and waiting for something good to happen. You've had an argument with Lorenzo and are feeling bitter. Just remember what made you fall in love in the first place. How would you feel if he was here now, sharing all of this with you? Would you look at anyone else, or would he be everything to you? You have to weigh up the short term with the long term and I'm sure you will see things aren't that much better."

Her eyes fill up again and she takes a sip of her margarita. "It's not just an argument. We've been having a lot of them lately. I can't seem to do anything right and he appears disappointed with me. I have tried to fit in, but his family is so close. They make me welcome, of course they do, they are lovely people; but I know they are disappointed in Lorenzo's choice. I'm too much of a free spirit to settle down so soon to family life. I want us to travel and experience things together, but he won't hear of it. Maybe all we have in common is lust and sex. That's not enough to build a solid foundation for a marriage - is it?"

Before I can answer, I do a double take. Nudging Rachel we look at the sight coming our way. If I didn't see legs underneath it all, I would think a huge moving, magical carpet was heading our way. Escorting it through the sun-kissed bodies lying worshipping the sun is Marcus, looking very pleased with himself.

Rachel looks as confused as I am as they stop before us. I gesture to the carpet mountain.

"What's going on, Marcus? Is this your new business or something? Surely things aren't so bad that you must resort to bed to bed selling for your tequila money."

Marcus grins and wags his finger at me.

"Now, now, Becca, this isn't anything to do with me. Underneath all this woven cotton is Elvis. He has been charged with distributing Mexico's finest Artisan crafted rugs to all the poor sick sailors from yesterday's boat trip. They are by way of an apology from Captain Elviras who was inconsolable with grief that we didn't enjoy his trip of a lifetime. Just pick one each and we can carry on."

I look at Rachel and she shakes her head in amazement.

"I'll never get this in my Samsonite luggage. Tell him it's fine, I couldn't possibly accept such a kind gift."

Marcus looks annoyed.

"It would be insulting to him to refuse. Even if you have to fashion a uniform out of it like in the Sound of Music, you're having one and be grateful for it."

Rachel rolls her eyes.

"Ok, I'll have the one on the top to save Elvis from a rug avalanche."

I smile incredulously.

"I'll have the next one. Tell your uncle that we are extremely grateful and not to worry at all about the trip. It wasn't his fault that the sea wasn't very hospitable yesterday."

I hear a mumbled response from underneath the stack and then watch with amusement as they carry on with their mission.

Rachel grins. "What are we going to do with these? I must say, I quite like mine, actually. I'm sure it would look lovely in my conservatory."

I have to agree. "Yes, they do have a certain charm about them. Maybe Pete will let us stow them in the hold. One thing about being crew you don't have to worry about baggage allowance."

Rachel snorts. "Yes, do you remember when we bought a bike each in Orlando? The looks we got as we pushed the boxes through customs. I think every member of the crew bought one on that trip."

I grin. "Yes, the trouble was when we unpacked them they were all in pieces. It cost me a lot more to get the local wheelies bike shop to put it together. Not to mention that I had to put it on eBay a few months later because it was taking up valuable space in my lobby. Sometimes a bargain isn't really a bargain after all."

Rachel giggles.

"Yes, what about that CD player I bought in Miami? I completely forgot that the plugs and voltage were different, and it was useless at home. It was a total waste of money."

Laughing, I roll my eyes. Despite everything, we have a great life and I can see why Rachel doesn't want to give this up. Despite the mundane job, this life is exciting in a lot of ways. Anything else would seem dull to memories like these.

I look at her with concern.

"Will you be ok, Rachel? What will happen if you can't work things out with Lorenzo?"

She shrugs sadly.

"I don't know. I was brought up to believe that marriage is for keeps. You work at it and resolve your problems and move on happier for it. I never thought it would be this hard. We've only been married for a few months and I'm already looking for flats to rent in estate agent's windows and wondering if I could afford them on my own. That's not normal, is it? Surely, we should still be in the honeymoon period. It's as if my life is on fast-forward. What if Lorenzo doesn't turn out to be my Prince Charming, and it ends up that I've kissed a frog instead?"

She gulps her cocktail miserably and I don't have an answer to her question. I am running out of good advice and platitudes. The problem is greater than I first realised.

~*~*~*~*~

Chapter 27

We spend the rest of the day sunbathing. I think we are all exhausted and far from being a restful trip, this has turned into party central. I enjoy spending my day with Luke beside me. We enjoy taking refreshing dips in the pool together and by the end of the day, I feel as if I have known him for ages. We feel comfortable around each other and have fallen into an easy relationship.

It must be about 3pm when Jo and Pete finally make an appearance. They walk towards us holding hands and looking very pleased with themselves. Jo smiles at us all as she places her towel on the other side of Rachel.

"So, what did we miss?"

I laugh. "Nothing but a day of relaxation and gifts from Captain Elviras."

She raises her eyes and we quickly fill her in.

Pete looks over and grins.

"We'll find a corner for them in the hold. That was kind of him, he didn't have to do that."

Rachel nods. "It was sweet. I suppose at least we will have a nice memento of our trip. A bit like Mr Ben used to. I loved that bit at the end when he always found a memento of his adventure in his pocket."

Luke laughs. "I loved that cartoon. I always wanted to find the changing room and go out the other side into an adventure."

We giggle and look up in astonishment as Jenny races over, looking as if she has just run a marathon. Jo says loudly, "What's happened to you, Jenny? You look exhausted."

She rolls her eyes.

"We had a party of twenty for para-gliding. I've been at it for most of the day. Flynn is just putting everything away and said I should come and grab some rest. It's certainly exhausting working non-stop all day in this heat."

Rachel looks thoughtful.

"This would be your life. Are you sure you could do it day in day out?"

Jenny nods emphatically.

"As long as I'm with Flynn, I don't care if I work 24/7. The thought of leaving him in a couple of days is tearing my heart out. I can't believe we have to give a month's notice. It will seem like agony."

Looking over at Luke he catches my eye and nods sadly. Yes, I share Jenny's concerns. The trouble is, her one month is six to us. How can I bear to be away from him for so long?

It must be an hour later that Luke jumps up and holds out his hand.

"Fancy a walk along the beach, Becca?"

I smile up at him and take his hand quickly. As if I'm about to turn down a romantic stroll with this love god, tempting me with his body at every twist and turn in the day.

We leave the others to it and start the slow walk along the sand. The beach is quite busy, and it isn't the dreamy experience I thought it would be. I had hoped we could find rare shells. Then we would make matching love necklaces, binding us together for all eternity. All we find are lots of locals trying to sell us things that we don't need or want. After about fifteen minutes, Luke growls angrily.

"Come on, let's head back and grab a drink. At least we won't be pestered there."

I nod miserably. "Surely the hotel should have a private beach for our enjoyment. It's meant to be one of the best. If I was a star giver by trade, I would deduct one of their five for this outrage."

Luke laughs, and grabs hold of me playfully. "That is what I love about you, Becca. You say the strangest things in the sweetest way. I never know what is going on in that crazy mind of yours."

Ok, let's just take a moment and rewind this conversation. "THAT IS WHAT I LOVE ABOUT YOU." Luke said the love word. He may not have meant it literally, but I'll take it. In love with Luke. Luke and Becca in love. I love you, Becca. I love you, Luke. Why is it so important to a person to hear those words? I know it was just a figure of speech, but it has left a warm glow inside me.

Luke grins and pulls me close, kissing me in full view of everyone on the beach. How I must be the envy of every red-blooded woman here. I kiss him back with a passion I never knew I had. Dreams don't come better than this. Dreams have a habit of changing into really weird events though. I mean, in my dreams Luke would be kissing me like this and would then change into *Brick Man* or *First-Class man*. Then we would be living in the jungle with the apes or something. No, this dream is reality, for a few more days at least and they can't pass slowly enough for me. I never want this to end.

We are eating at the hotel tonight before our party with the Queen's men later. It's funny how my room has become a sort of meeting room to get ready in and Luke's has become, what it is, our Love Palace. He watches me apply my make up while leaning back on the bed, looking far too tempting to be allowed out for his own safety.

"You know, Becca, I never thought I'd meet someone like you. It's funny how things work out, isn't it?"

I nod. "It sure is. Just think, if your brother had got married we would never have never met. Quite a scary thought when you think of it. Life is a lot about fate, isn't it?"

He looks thoughtful.

"Yes. I wonder if this was fate intervening and taking us down a different path. I mean, look at Jenny. Her life has changed so much in the few short days she has been here. It's like watching someone on fast-forward. Do you really think she will give it all up and move out here?"

I shake my head. "Who knows? Things have a habit of changing when you return to the familiar. Out here we are in a bubble. Ordinary life is left at home and we get to experience the freedom of those with no cares or worries. You have to return to face it sometime though and that's what's worrying me the most. What if things change and we lose the joy of this moment? It's not a nice thought is it?"

I sit down heavily next to him and he turns my face to look at him. My breath catches as I see the look in his eyes. He says softly.

"We will make sure we keep what we have alive. I may have to return to sea but this time I will be taking you with me in my heart. I can bear the endless days cooped up in that pressure cooker if I know that you are my prize on my return. The trouble is, I'm not sure that you'll want to wait for me. It's a lot to ask and I have no right to ask it of you."

Once again, I see the worry in his eyes and trace his face with my fingers, kissing him gently on the lips.

"I've waited a long time for this, Luke. Corny I know, but true. Six months is nothing. Even if you only get one day off in six months, it will be worth the wait. You don't get rid of me that easily."

Luke's eyes shine, and he lowers his lips to mine. "Then we shouldn't waste a minute more."

I think I glide into the restaurant one hour later with Luke's hand tightly in mine. Wow, what an hour that was. My feelings for him are growing by the second, if that's possible. We see the others sipping cocktails at a large table and take the last two seats. Jo winks and grins knowingly.

"You took your time."

I grin and roll my eyes.

"Sorry guys, something came up. Have you ordered already?"

They laugh and thrust the menus towards us. "Yes, so hurry up. We're starving here."

It doesn't take long before our food arrives. Luke is chatting to Flynn, so I turn to Jo and smile.

"I'm glad to see that you made things up with Pete. You must be so relieved."

She nods happily. "Yes, I can't believe I let it get to me so much. Pete is definitely the one for me. In fact, we have even started planning our wedding already."

Gosh, they don't hang around. She smiles. "Yes. We've chosen the venue and as soon as we return I'm going to see what dates they have available. I would love a summer wedding and Pete agrees."

I lower my voice.

"Um... about your... um ... condition. Won't that dictate the dates for you?"

Jo looks a little sad. "Not really. It turned out to be a false alarm. I suppose it was the stress I was under keeping me from being regular. Now that stress has gone so has the dream of a baby."

I look at her sad face and say softly.

"I'm sorry. You were both so happy at the thought. You would make lovely parents."

She smiles sadly.

"One day we will. Once we are married, we will try non-stop until our family starts to grow. It's probably best this way. It means we can have our wedding first and then think about our life together."

She looks around with excitement and says loudly.

"Listen, girls, talking about the wedding. I was wondering if you would all be my bridesmaids."

The shrieks are deafening as we squeal madly. The guys laugh as we look at Jo with excitement.

She laughs. "I'll take that as a yes. Now, remember, as my bridesmaids you will be involved in everything. We will have to go dress shopping, plan a fabulous hen night and do lots of girly wedding stuff."

I nod happily. This is right up my street. I love a good wedding and am more than happy to dive head first into this one. Jenny looks worried.

"I would love to, but you may have to leave me out. I will be out here and won't be able to fulfil my duties. I would obviously come back for the wedding but I'm not sure I'll be able to afford to come back multiple times."

Jo rolls her eyes.

"Of course, you must be one. It doesn't matter if you can't be there for everything. I want you there on the one day that counts and that's good enough for me."

The rest of the meal is spent discussing the upcoming nuptials and I almost feel sorry for the guys. They must be so bored as we chatter away incessantly. They soon talk amongst themselves and leave us to it.

~*~*~*~*~

Chapter 28

We are soon back at the ship and the excitement radiating off of every person here is palpable.

We contemplate the beast in front of us and wonder what the night will bring.

Almost as soon as we step foot on board, I notice that Mark comes rushing up, smiling.

"You made it. It's good of you to come."

Pete smiles. "Thanks for asking us. Hopefully, we won't cause a drama tonight."

Mark laughs and looks at Jo.

"How are you feeling today after your experience last night?"

She just laughs and squeezes Pete's hand.

"Like a new woman, actually. Fainting was the best thing that could have happened to me."

He grins, and I watch as his eyes zone in on Rachel. A look passes between them and the warning bells ring loudly around me. Oh no, that look is trouble for everyone involved. Maybe this wasn't such a good idea.

I watch helplessly as he moves across and whispers something to her.

She throws her head back and laughs and gazes at him with the look of a woman very much interested in what stands before her. I feel the blood rushing to my head as I picture poor Lorenzo washing dishes in the restaurant, while his wife gets cosy with a fit sailor. No wonder he wants her to give this up.

Luke whispers, "Come on Becca, I'll grab you a drink."

We head towards the officer's mess where the party is underway. Most of our crew are now attacking the ship's bar. The atmosphere is different to last night. Tonight, appears more relaxed and the uniforms have been replaced with more casual attire, failing to disguise the hotness of the men wearing it. They may be dressed as regular guys, but they are still hot men in uniform. Surely every girls' dream come true.

I notice many female sailors are here and I whisper to Luke, "How many sailorettes are normally at sea? Do they have their own wing of the ship, or do they have to bunk up with the men?"

Luke laughs loudly and pulls me close, whispering,

"Firstly, they are sailors, not sailorettes. You may want to amend that entry in the Thesaurus. Secondly, it's against the ship's law to bunk up together. The women have their own, all-female cabins, and just work alongside the men. They would hate it any other way."

I grin and allow him to pull me close as a slow song comes on. Once again, we hug dance in the middle of the officer's mess, not caring who sees us. Jo and Pete are also dancing in a similar way and Jenny and Flynn are doing their usual sex dance to entertain the gaping crowd. Soon others join in and as the ship gently rocks I allow myself to be held by my very own anchor. Luke keeps me from harm as the ship rolls with the waves. I close my eyes and savour the feeling of his hard body pressed against mine. The trouble is, when I open them again, I see the sight I was dreading. Swaying nearby and so close you couldn't get a finger between them are Rachel and Mark. They are hug dancing with the rest of us and her head is on his shoulder and his hands are rubbing circles on her back. Code red, Defcon three, world war 3 is about to break out, man overboard and what the hell? Rachel is playing a dangerous game and I know the fallout will be huge.

I must stiffen because Luke looks around to see what I can see. I hiss, "What's she playing at? Has she left all morality back in London? I can't believe my eyes."

Luke looks concerned. "Mark should know better. He knows she's married and should stay away. I'll have a word if you like."

Shaking my head, I sigh. "It's not our place to play parents to Rachel. She's a grown woman and can make her own mistakes. I know she's hurting but I can't condone what she is doing. When you get married in my opinion, it's for keeps and there should be no room for passengers."

Luke pulls back and says huskily.

"I'm glad to hear that. I feel the same. What's the point of marriage if you give yourself the odd hall pass here and there? It should be a lifetime commitment, despite the problems it may throw up. Don't get me wrong, if it doesn't work out then I wouldn't blame anyone for calling it quits and moving on. You should be honest up to then though and stay faithful. It doesn't include slow dancing with a sailor who obviously has a lot more than that on his mind."

I look at him in horror.

"You don't think they would… um… you know…?"

Luke pulls a face. "Who knows? Like you say, it's a bit of a bubble out here, for them as much as us. These guys are locked up together for months at a time. Mark won't be thinking about Rachel's situation at all. He is way past that point. He is just concerned that he has a hot woman in his arms and won't want to pass up on the opportunity."

I don't know why but warning bell starts ringing in my head. I wonder if Luke would feel the same in similar circumstances. Maybe this is what life is like dating a member of the armed forces. Accepting that they may stray when the urge takes them. I'm not sure I could bear that.

I keep it in and just try to enjoy the time we do have. Maybe it won't be my problem anyway when we return to London. Luke may sail away and never return - to me anyway. Pushing the unwelcome thought away, I just try to relax and enjoy the evening.

Soon the drink takes hold, and the party is in full swing. Marcus and Elvis are out of control and having the time of their life. It appears that one or two of the sailors on board are more than happy to party with them both, making all of Marcus's dreams come true. I just enjoy spending time with Luke and try to absorb the whole experience to keep me warm when I return home.

I suppose it must be a couple of hours later that I get chatting with a couple of female sailors at the bar. Luke is laughing and joking with a crowd of guys nearby and Rachel and I are grabbing a drink. I smile at the friendly face of one of the girls and she smiles back.

"Hi, I'm Samantha and this is Kate."

I introduce Rachel and I and look at them with interest.

"It must be exciting working on this ship."

Kate grins.

"It has its perks."

Samantha rolls her eyes.

"More like pitfalls. The trouble is, these guys are out of control most of the time. If you let one of them in you live out a whole relationship in a matter of weeks. They never last though."

I look at them with a worried expression.

"What do you mean, they don't last?"

Kate snorts.

"There's nowhere to go on here. It's hard having a relationship with someone under this microscope. A lot of them do but they rarely work out. As soon as we return home they seem to fizzle out."

Samantha shakes her head.

"Not all of them. I've known many a sailor wedding. The hardest thing is making it work if you get posted on another ship."

Kate grins.

"Mainly they let the married couples stay together but sometimes it doesn't work out. No, mark my words, never marry a sailor. In fact, don't even trust them because the temptation thrown their way at every opportunity doesn't make them the most loyal partners out there."

My warning bells are now deafening me and I can see that Rachel is feeling uncomfortable at the turn the conversation is taking.

The girls laugh. "Look at them. They don't have a care in the world."

We look over and see the group of guys laughing and joking nearby.

Kate sighs irritably.

"It's ok for them. They have the life of Riley. The girls fall at their feet dropping their knickers on the way down. When you're a female sailor, things are very different. Most normal guys don't want to date a woman doing a man's job. Especially as she spends most of her life cooped up with the likes of them. It's no wonder most of us get sucked in by their fellow sailors. There's no other option."

I am starting to feel a little green around the edges in every way. I wish they would stop but they carry on, their words shattering my happiness by the second.

Samantha laughs. "Yes, they certainly talk the talk. I've known them promise a girl the world to have their moment of fun and then as soon as they head back to sea she is forgotten. If they haven't found a better alternative by the time they return, she may get another shot out of him, but it probably won't be for long."

She shakes her head sadly. "I pity any poor girl who loses her heart to a sailor."

Rachel is quiet and if anything good has come out of this conversation, it's that I hope it brings her to her senses. Me on the other hand, well, I'm devastated. The euphoria of my relationship is being battered by the grim realisation that they are probably right. I suppose I have known it all along. Of course, this won't last. I was a fool for thinking it would. I have known Luke for a few days and dropped my knickers, as they so kindly put it, quicker than a respectable girl has every right doing. I feel ashamed of myself for thinking that I was different. Luke is just passing the time with a willing partner before he heads off again. I was so gullible in believing that it was more than it is. It's taken the words of those who know to bring me to my senses.

~*~*~*~*~

Chapter 29

The rest of the evening passes in a blur. I try not to let their words affect me but I'm only human. I give myself a stern talking to and decide that if it is the case, then so what. Now I know what to expect it will make the inevitable easier. Like Luke, I will just enjoy the ride for the few short days we have left. When we part we will part as friends and I won't expect any more of him. Yes, that's my plan of action. Use Luke for sex and then head home to Malcolm an empowered, modern day woman.

Then why do I feel crushed, bruised and battered and as though someone has died?

It must be the early hours of the morning when we leave the ship. We have arranged to meet up with a group of the sailors tomorrow - or should I say today, to go to a nearby beach they know of. Apparently, it has hammocks strung up in front of the ocean and hardly anybody goes there. Once again, I worry about Rachel as I watch Mark kiss her goodbye. It's only a brief kiss, more like a friend than a lover, but I don't miss the lingering of his lips on her cheek or the sparkle in her eyes.

I'm quiet on the way back to the hotel and Luke whispers, "Are you ok, Becca? You've been uncharacteristically quiet this evening."

I smile as brightly as I can when my heart is broken. "Just tired I think. It's been quite full on these last few days."

He puts his arm around me and pulls me close, whispering,

"Let's get you to bed then. Maybe we should have a lie in and try to recharge our batteries. I agree it's been exhausting."

Trying to fight back the tears, I hate the fact that I love his arm around me. I know it won't be for much longer and I am very close to crying uncontrollably for what I'm about to lose. It would appear those girls were right. I have lived out a relationship in just a few short days. Now I am coping with the inevitable break up and planning on leaving the love of my life before we've even got started. Just my luck to fall in love with the unattainable.

I wake up the next morning with a heavy heart. I slept fitfully as everything I heard rattled around my brain. This is the sweetest torture. I have it all and yet I have nothing. Part of me wishes I had never met Luke. Surely, it's better not to have loved at all than feel this huge loss heading my way.

I can tell that Luke is confused by my mood. He keeps on throwing me worried glances as we dive into the honeymoon breakfast. After about five minutes of stilted conversation, he fixes me with those sexy eyes that glitter with questions.

"Is everything ok, Becca? You haven't been yourself since we returned from the ship. Did something happen to upset you?"

Shaking my head, I try to smile brightly.

"No, of course not. Like I said, I was just tired. It's been a busy few days and I suppose I'm not used to it. Maybe a morning in a hammock on the beach will perk me up again."

Luke looks unconvinced but smiles softly.

"I hope they can fit two people in them because I want to be with you every minute we have left."

I nod emphatically. "Me too. Anyway, let's not dwell on the inevitable. We still have two more days to enjoy ourselves. Let's make the most of them."

Grinning, he pulls me up. "Come on then. Your wish is my command."

After a very harrowing taxi ride, we pull up at the lonely beach. However, it's not so lonely anymore as about five taxis deposit their load and roar off leaving us all stranded.

We follow the others to the beach and I gasp in amazement as Rachel squeals with excitement.

"Oh my goodness. This is amazing. Come on Becca, I'll race you to a hammock."

As I set off after her I share her joy. Lonely beach, unlike dirty beach, is set up for a day of fun in the sand. Various hammocks swing gently from a covered wooden gazebo type thing and the white sand stretches for miles. The sea sparkles in the sunlight, and the whole place reeks of Robinson Crusoe. There is a little beachfront bar a short walking distance away and like its name suggests, we appear to be the only inhabitants.

As well as some of our crew, there are also various sailors milling around. A few of them have set up a volleyball net and are hard at it on the sand. Some raced off into the sea and a few are at the bar already.

Jo and Pete catch us up and she smiles happily.

"Look at this place, it's amazing."

I nod in agreement.

"It certainly is. We are in for a good day."

Looking around, I don't see Jenny anywhere and turn to Jo.

"Is Jenny not coming?"

She shrugs. "No, they have a lot of customers today and couldn't spare the time."

I feel disappointed. I'm glad that Jenny met Flynn, I really am, but I also feel as if I haven't seen half of much of her as I would have liked. She should be resting, not swapping one job for another.

Rachel sees my expression and whispers.

"Don't worry about Jenny. Flynn is all she wants and if he is making her happy then we should be too. Of all of us, she deserves bucket loads of it after the last two years of sadness and pain."

I nod, feeling selfish.

"You're right, Rachel. I just wanted us to be all together. We don't have much longer and if Jenny does leave, then we won't be seeing her for a long time."

Suddenly, I hear,

"Rachel, over here."

We look in the direction of the voice and my heart sinks as I see Mark waving her over. He appears to have acquired a double hammock and I watch in horror as she races over and jumps in with him. Luke leans down and whispers,

"She'll be fine. We'll keep an eye on them. I'm sure she won't do anything she'll regret later on. Anyway, we had better grab one of those ourselves if we don't want to lie on the sand like the last beach we went to."

Trying to shake off my sinking feeling, I follow him to the hammock hut.

After the third attempt I look at the hammock as if it's my worst enemy. Putting my hands on my hips, I glare at Luke who is laughing uncontrollably as he watches me.

"It's not funny. These things are death traps."

I rub my knee as I say it. Three times I have fallen out of it and now I feel like a child in the playground with a scraped knee. The others are laughing as they swing in their hammocks while looking at us with smug expressions.

Then, Luke grabs me in one superhero move and places me carefully in the swinging death trap.

I look at him in surprise. "Why didn't you do that in the first place?"

He laughs. "Because it was much more fun watching you trying to get in. I haven't seen such a sight since ... actually, I don't think I've ever seen such a sight."

He strips off his t-shirt, and it was worth the trouble because I could look at that body all day. He is super fit and now tanned and toned. I wonder if it's rude to openly stare at his body like I'm doing. I can't help myself, it's just too perfect.

He jumps in to join me and the hammock swings dangerously. Shrieking, I try to reach out and steady us but only manage to pull on Rachel and Mark's one.

Rachel shouts, "Hey, get off, Becca. Just because you fell out, it doesn't mean that you can try to do the same to us."

I grin at them. "Sorry. I'm sure I'll get the hang of it soon."

Once Luke has settled in we all lie swinging in the breeze surrounded by paradise. How on earth did I deserve this?

I look around at the spectacle before my eyes. Hot sailors frolicking in the sand, all bare-chested and oozing sex appeal. A glorious beach paradise set up for our pleasure and the hottest sunny day to relax our mind and bodies. I am flanked by my best friends and sitting opposite me rubbing my feet is the sexiest man alive.

Luke smiles at me happily.

"It doesn't get much better than this, does it, Becca?"

My heart lifts as I see the look in his eyes. "Surely he isn't just spinning me a well-used line. Maybe those girls were wrong. Luke is my future, I'm sure of it."

I'm conscious of Rachel and Mark getting on well beside us. For the first time this trip she is laughing as if she hasn't a care in the world. He is obviously charming the pants off her and once again I worry about my friend. Jo and Pete are talking about the wedding and I listen in with interest as I close my eyes and swing in the breeze. Jo sounds very excited.

"You know, I've always wanted a big wedding, Pete. All of my family and friends watching us pledge our life together in an amazing stately home. I actually can't wait to get home and get started with the planning."

Pete appears to be sleeping but grunts in all the right places. Jo carries on. "We must go and see the vicar of that lovely little church we saw in Brockham. You know, the one in Four Weddings and a Funeral. Either that or the one in Shere. It's so pretty and I would love to get married somewhere famous. I mean, I know Westminster Abbey is out, so surely it's the next best thing."

Pete just grunts, and Luke nudges me. I stifle a grin as Jo turns to Rachel and me.

"You know, girls, we must all arrange to go dress shopping as soon as possible. I was thinking cornflower blue silk for your dresses and of course I will wear white. I'll set up an appointment with Dream Days as soon as we get home."

I look at her in surprise.

"What's Dream Days when it's at home?"

Jo looks excited.

"It's a wedding planning service. They arrange everything you want and leave nothing to chance. They have discounts at various bridal shops and know all the best florists and party organisers. I am so getting me a wedding planner like they do in the movies. I only intend on doing this once, so it has to be utterly amazing. Isn't that right, Pete?"

Pete just grunts, and I wonder if he has registered anything she has said. He appears to be dozing and probably thinks he's dreaming. Well, he's in for a rude awakening when he has to get his wallet out. By the sounds of it, Jo is fast turning into Bridezilla and I pity him the rough time ahead.

After an hour of relaxation, Luke nods towards the bar. "Do you fancy grabbing a drink with me, Becca?"

Looking at the ground with trepidation, I grimace.

"Only if you lift me out of this contraption. I'm not sure it's safe if I'm left to my own devices."

Actually, I think I could get out quite easily, but am using it as an excuse to be secured in Luke's arms for a few more minutes.

I savour the feeling of his hard-toned body holding me carefully against him as he lifts me with ease. Rachel catches my eye and grins as I wink at her. She rolls her eyes and giggles. She knows me so well.

Luke and I head off towards the bar holding hands. A brief fling, or a lifetime together? I don't care because at this moment I am the happiest girl on the planet.

~*~*~*~*~

Chapter 30

I think that Lonely Beach is my favourite place in the world. We've had a marvellous day. After our trip to the bar where we sipped cocktails and ate a nice lunch, we headed back to the death trap hammocks for a siesta.

Then we spent a nice hour playing volleyball and messing around in the sea. The guys were all great company and I don't think I've laughed so much - ever!

By the time we sink down in the seats of our taxi ride home, I have placed all thoughts of the inevitable out of my mind.

It's only when we return to the hotel that I realise Marcus wasn't with us. I notice that Elvis is working and looking strangely moody, so I head over to him.

"Hey, Elvis. Do you know where Marcus is?"

Shaking his head, he looks upset.

"He went to meet someone, and I haven't seen him all day."

I look at him in surprise.

"Who did he meet?"

He shrugs, looking annoyed.

"He met a gentleman in Los Romanticos last night. They were getting quite friendly, and he told me to leave without him. I tried to tell him that I would wait for him, but he said he was spending the night with this man and would see me this morning."

An icy hand grips my heart as I share a worried look with Luke.

"Haven't you seen him since?"

Elvis shakes his head miserably.

"No, but I'm worried about him, Becca. I asked my Cousin, Enrique, who works there if he saw him leave and he said they left about 4 am. He doesn't know where they went because he has never seen the man before."

He looks at me with a stricken expression.

"Do you think I should call the police?"

Now I'm really worried. How did I not notice that Marcus was missing? Today would have been his dream come true, and I was so wrapped up in my own despair that I completely took my eye off the ball.

I look at Luke with worry in my eyes.

"This doesn't seem right. What should we do?"

Luke takes charge like an officer of the Armed forces would.

"Elvis, call your contacts from the other hotels in the area. If this guy is a tourist, they may have gone to his hotel. Then get housekeeping to check his room, you never know they may have returned here, and you just missed him. Once that is all done we can decide where to go from here. We may need to file a missing person report and should cover all possibilities first if we want to be taken seriously. While you're at it, think about anyone you know who was there last night and phone them. You never know, they may have some information."

He smiles as he sees our stricken expressions.

"Don't worry. I'm sure Marcus is fine. He can take care of himself and is probably sleeping off the effects of a wild night out."

From the look on Elvis's face, he's not convinced. I don't think I am either. Marcus should know better than to go off with a stranger from a bar, especially in a foreign land. This spells trouble on every level.

Luke and I head out to the pool and decide to wait it out there. As we reach the sunbeds, I notice that Jenny is stretched out with Flynn beside her. They appear to be fast asleep and I smile. They look such a cute couple. I'm so glad that Jenny found him.

We spread out our towels next to them and Jenny sits up looking sleepy.

"Hey, guys. How was the beach?"

Smiling broadly, I tell her every last delicious detail. Then I remember Marcus and tell her what I know.

She looks worried. "Oh no, do you think he's ok? I've heard of terrible things happening to Brits abroad. What if this guy is a murderer or has Marcus bound and gagged in a dungeon somewhere?"

Pushing the thought away that Marcus would probably be having the time of his life if that was the case, I return her worried look.

"Elvis is ringing around. I'm sure he'll be fine. Marcus is a big boy, he can look after himself."

Flynn sits up and looks at us with a worried look.

"I'll ask around. I know quite a few people who may have seen something. If they've been to the beach today, we'll soon know about it."

I look at him gratefully as he springs into action. Jenny looks at him gratefully.

"Thanks, honey. Do you want me to come with you?"

Flynn's eyes soften, and he kisses her gently on the lips.

"No, you stay here, possum. You've worked so hard you deserve the rest. I won't be long, anyway."

As she watches him go, Jenny sighs.

"I can't believe I met Flynn. I think my mum must have sent him to me from heaven because he is everything I ever wanted."

I smile at her.

"Yes, we've been very lucky this week, haven't we?"

Jenny looks at Luke and grins.

"What about you two? What are your plans when you get home?"

I think I'm holding my breath as Luke smiles at me adoringly. He takes my hand and kissing it gently says, "I'm not letting this one out of my sight until I have to leave again. I'm kidnapping Becca and taking her to Somerset to meet my parents. Then we will spend what's left of our time together locked in my room and she will only be allowed out to eat."

Jenny laughs and says with interest.

"How long will you be away?"

I find that I'm holding my breath as Jenny unknowingly asks the questions I lack the courage to ask.

"Luke's face clouds over and he says despondently.

"Three months this time. Unfortunately, I used up my leave allowance for my brother's wedding. It will be back to work with a vengeance and may be some time before I can get more time off. I don't want to leave Becca though."

Jenny looks at us with sympathy, but I listen to Luke's words on repeat in my brain. Maybe he's setting me up for the inevitable fall. Maybe Kate and Samantha were right and he's using his 'get out of potential relationship with a neurotic woman' jail free card. I will be used and abused and left pining for what could have been.

Luke looks as miserable as I feel, and Jenny laughs nervously.

"Well, I'm sure you will work something out. I mean, look at me. Who would have thought my life would change so dramatically in such a short space of time? I'm hoping to return here after I hand in my notice. I only have to give a month, so it shouldn't be too long to wait. I'm also going to see if I can swap with someone who is on the next trip out here. Even if I must pay them, it would be worth it. So, you see, with a little manoeuvring you can make your dreams come true."

She settles back on her sunbed and looks extremely satisfied. Luke and I share a look and if it's any consolation, he looks as devastated as I am.

~*~*~*~

Chapter 31

By the time we meet up for pre-dinner drinks Marcus is still not back. There was no answer from his room which was annoying because he still hosts the crew party room. Instead, we congregate in the bar and I fill the others in on what happened. Pete looks worried.

"I think I should contact the police. This isn't right, and it's my duty to look out for my crew. Leave it with me and I'll ask reception to contact the police."

He heads off with a worried looking Jo and Rachel looks at us with concern. "What do you think happened?"

Flynn shrugs.

"I asked around at the beach and nobody could tell me anything. It's as if he has vanished into thin air."

I can see Elvis across the polished marble floor in reception looking miserable and my heart sinks. Poor Elvis. They struck up quite the friendship, and he is obviously as worried about Marcus as we are. I nod towards him and Luke and I head over to see what he knows.

As he sees us coming, his face falls even further, if that's possible.

I whisper, "Hey, Elvis, have you heard anything?"

Shaking his head, he lowers his voice.

"No, nobody knows who this man is. He is a stranger that only appeared in the bar last night. He doesn't appear to be staying in any of the hotels around here and, yet they didn't get a taxi because my cousin Romero runs the local taxi company."

Fleetingly, I wonder if Elvis has a relation in every establishment in Acapulco. Shaking my head, I look at Luke with a worried expression.

"This isn't like Marcus. He's wild but not irresponsible. What do you think happened?"

Luke shakes his head.

"I'm not sure, but if I know Marcus he'll be fine. He's probably having the time of his life and completely unaware of this storm brewing."

After making Elvis promise to let us know if he finds anything out we head back to the bar.

While we wait for Pete and Jo I decide to question Rachel on her developing friendship with Mark. Luke heads off to order us some drinks, so I waste no time.

"So, madam, what's the story with Mark?"

I don't miss the light that sparkles in her eyes as she sighs heavily.

"He's amazing isn't he, Becca? If I wasn't a married woman I would be in there like a shot."

I feel myself relax at her words. Thank goodness for one worry resolved. I smile gently.

"Have you thought any more about Lorenzo and your situation?"

She shakes her head looking sad again.

"I called him when I got back from the beach. It was like talking to a stranger. He was cold and abrupt, and the conversation was stilted."

Reaching out, I grab her hand and squeeze it gently.

"How did you leave it?"

She shakes her head sadly.

"It was so awkward. It was as though we were strangers. Neither of us said much and I think he just wanted to go. There were no declarations of love and I didn't feel like making them myself. I wanted to see if the sound of his voice would push away my worries and concerns. Unfortunately, they only magnified them. Just before he hung up he said in a cold voice that we would talk when I returned. There was much to discuss and if this marriage was going to work sacrifices were going to have to be made. Then somebody called him and he said he had to go. He hung up, and it left me with an empty feeling."

She looks upset and says brokenly.

"It was as if we were strangers, not lovers. How did it get to this?"

I have no words left to comfort her. Whatever I say will seem empty. The only way this will be resolved is when she returns home and talks it through with her husband. Poor Rachel, like me she must be dreading returning home.

For the first time since we arrived, dinner is a sombre affair. Even the usual shots of tequila do nothing to lift our morale and as the hours tick by with no sight or sound of Marcus our worry increases. Where is he?

We eat with the crew in a lovely local restaurant, near to the English bar. After listening to Jo speak incessantly about the wedding all night, I am decidedly in the mood to get wasted in the bar afterwards.

As we head inside it appears to be Karaoke night, as the dulcet tones of a man in a Union Jack t-shirt greets us as we head inside.

We are all subdued as we sit contemplating the situation.

However, after several tequilas, we are soon hogging the microphone.

Jenny and Flynn sing the Jason and Kylie duet and have us in stitches. They look so adorable together, despite the huge tattoos of their own stupidity glaring out at us. I hope she doesn't live to regret that very rash decision.

Then Jo and I head up and sing Mama Mia. My life appears to be dominated by Abba tracks. Luke jumps up and does a rendition of Mustang Sally and then Rachel sings, Love Me Like You do, by Ellie Goulding. I try to shake off the knowledge that she stares at Mark sexily the whole time as she sings it. This trip is proving to be one big anxiety filled nightmare in so many ways. Maybe I should seek out the Great Ernesto and get myself hypnotised. It worked so well for Jenny. I think her anxious ways were transferred over to me instead.

We head back to the hotel and decide to call it a night. We leave Pete and Jo to talk to the hotel receptionist about filing a missing person's report and Luke and I head back to our Love Palace.

The roses are off the scale tonight and the only consolation is so are the little chocolate love hearts. We sit in the bath, like we did on that first night and eat chocolates and drink champagne as we watch the stars twinkling all around the bay.

Luke kisses the top of my head as I sit with his arm around me and my head on his shoulder. He whispers,

"We'll work something out, Becca. Now that I've found you I don't want to let my job get in our way. If you'll have me that is. You may be sick of the sight of me already for all I know."

I lift my head and look into those sexy eyes and smile.

"I may be mad, Luke, but I'm not stupid. How will I ever get tired of having you in my life?"

Then we kiss so sweetly and then so passionately that any worries I have disappear into the air with the champagne bubbles. This is where I want to be, with Luke's arms around me and his lips on mine. The rest can wait. I'll deal with that when it happens.

~*~*~*~*~

Chapter 32

Our last day!

I wake up next to Luke for the last full day of our trip. My heart feels heavy and I wonder what will happen when this bubble bursts.

I feel him stir beside me and look into the love mirror and savour the sight of his body next to mine. That view will never get old and I need to imprint it on my memory just in case my worst fears come true. This may be the last time I see such a love god squashed beside me.

Luke stirs and pulls me close, nuzzling my neck in sleepy satisfaction.

"Hm, my favourite way to start the day - you."

My heart beats rapidly as I try to push the doubts from my mind. We have one more day of his brother's honeymoon to enjoy and I don't want to waste a minute.

By the time we finally surface from the love bed we are famished. I think we devour every item of the complimentary breakfast which we eat decadently in bed. I no longer care about the crumbs situation. I have even got used to the ever-present rose petals. It has been very difficult to stop myself from gathering them up to take home and make a Luke scented pot-pourri out of them. I know it's all about diffusers these days, but I wouldn't want to lie on one of those sticks all night. No, rose petals are now my friend. I intend on gathering as many of them as possible to inhale at every opportune moment when I'm back in my spinster flat for one and a potted plant.

As I shower and change, Luke leans against the tiled, Borgia inspired, wall of the bathroom and watches me. He seems preoccupied and my anxiety levels increase. Maybe he has sobered up and is seeing me in my real state. State being the operative word. Perhaps I should have ordered a tequila chaser for our croissant to keep the fantasy alive.

Feeling self-conscious, I smile nervously.

"Ae you ok, Luke? You seem to have something on your mind."

He nods and moves across the room and pulls me into his arms. He holds me close and says softly.

"Spend the day alone with me, Becca. There is a trip we could take to Taxco. They make silver jewellery there - in fact, they are famous for it. We could take in the true sights of Mexico and soak up the culture. Maybe even grab some lunch and make a lovely memory of our trip.

My heart leaps and I look at him with excitement. "I would love that. I love shopping. In fact, I have been seriously deprived of it out here. It would be good to indulge in some retail therapy before we take to the skies once again. What a lovely idea."

Luke just grins as I finish getting ready. I feel like singing a little tune of happiness but stop myself just in time. Luke has heard more than enough of my singing voice; I don't want to leave him with that as a lasting impression.

It doesn't take long and once we have told the others of our plan and Elvis arranged for a taxi, we are soon pulling into the little Mexican Town. I sat holding Luke's hand for the whole journey and pretended we were married.

Soon we are walking around like true tourists and I am loving every minute.

The town is absolutely beautiful. There are little mosaic fountains to admire and beautiful old buildings. The town is bigger than I thought and appears to be centred around a beautiful old church - The Santa Prisca de Taxco.

Luke and I walk hand in hand and pose for many a photograph.

As we walk down the narrow streets, we look in many shop windows. One catches our eye and Luke drags me inside. We look around at the sweet little shop and I gasp at the beautiful jewellery on display. The assistant smiles and speaks in broken English.

"Welcome to Taxco. Are you looking for something special to take home with you?"

I smile and shake my head.

"Just looking. They are all beautiful though."

He nods and pulls out a lovely tray of necklaces. "We only use the finest silver here and our designs are famous around the world. If you like silver, then you are in the best place."

I nod in agreement. "I can see that. These necklaces are beautiful."

Luke grins. "Try one on, Becca. You may as well, you won't get another chance."

I look at the necklaces and choose one that catches my eye. It is a delicate silver cross. It's plain and simple and not ostentatious like some of the designs. As I place it around my neck, I admire my reflection in the nearby mirror.

"This is lovely. How much is it?"

The assistant looks at a list by the cash register.

"That one is 800 Pesos."

I think about it and weigh up the purchase in my head. Not a bad price and surely priceless as it comes with the memory of who was with me when I bought it.

Before I can speak, Luke says loudly, "We'll take it."

I watch in surprise as he pulls the money from his wallet and looks at me and winks.

"A little souvenir from our honeymoon."

I giggle as the assistant throws up his hands with joy.

"Congratulations. I can tell you will be together forever."

Luke slides his hand into mine and smiles sexily.

"Yes, I think that's a definite."

My heart races as I get carried along by their words. Those girls on the ship were so wrong about Luke. Ok, some sailors may be like that but obviously submariners are a different breed altogether. Luke is now officially mine forever. This necklace cements our love and like the silver it is made from, nothing can break it.

Lunch is an intimate affair, and we feed each other little bits of pleasure from each other's plates. We enjoy a nice wine and gaze into each other's eyes. The mood is relaxed and romantic and as last days go it's the best.

Luke pushes a stray strand of hair from my eyes and says softly.

"I'm going to miss you so much, Becca."

Ok, that is not what I want to dwell on. Anxiety suddenly comes back with a vengeance and I wonder what he means. Does he mean when he's at sea, or forever? Is this his subtle way of letting me down gently or is this the end of the line? He must see the confusion in my eyes because he smiles ruefully.

"I never imagined I would meet someone like you. Now I have, I don't want it to end. How can I return to my old life and leave you behind?"

I nod sadly.

"Me too. It's been a special week hasn't it?"

He nods. "The best. The memories will keep me going during the long nights ahead."

I look at him with interest.

"It must be a strange experience living under water. What made you choose that as a career option?"

Luke's eyes light up.

"I suppose I've always wanted to be in the armed forces. You know, I played it as a little boy and never grew up. War seemed exciting and the thought of a 9-5 job was never really me. I was also interested in building things and finding out how they worked. So, I merged my interests and here I am today. I don't know how I ended up on the submarine though. It just happened and once again it seemed exciting and like a dream."

He shakes his head and I see the light in his eyes dim.

"I never knew it would have a shelf life though."

Leaning forward, I say with interest.

"What do you mean? Can you only stay there for a few years before your body acclimatises, and you grow webbed feet?"

Luke laughs softly. "You and your imagination, Becca. No, the shelf life is not with the job, it's with me. I suppose I never really looked beyond the here and now. It takes a lot to make someone truly happy, and I have learned that you need to share your life with someone that matters. When my brother told me about his engagement, I was happy and a little envious of him. He had found that special someone and his life was set. I would never find that holy grail cooped up on a submarine. Life goes on and we just get to dip back into it occasionally. It's no life really, not if you want the dream of a family. One day I want that, Becca. A beautiful wife who I adore and the token two kids and a dog. I want to be a good husband and father and could never be that if I disappeared off for months at a time."

He looks at me with a determined look in his eyes.

"It's up to me to make that happen. My future is in my hands and I need to make changes to live the dream."

He reaches out and takes my hand in his and I feel my heart thumping in my chest as I sense the seriousness of the situation. He says huskily.

"I know I don't have the right to ask this of you, but will you give us a chance, Becca? I know that I have to leave almost as soon as I have found you but the thought of you in my life will give me hope for the future. I love your funny ways and that you make me laugh. You are also the most beautiful woman I have ever met. If you will just try to see where this leads us, I will be the happiest man alive."

I look at Luke in total shock. Me-beautiful! I sneak a look at his drink resting innocently on the table in front of us and wonder if the waiter sneaked a tequila in there. Luke must be under the influence because we all know that I am no beauty. In fact, I am the strangest woman alive. I say and do things that most normal people would consider grounds for admittance to an asylum. I am paranoid and neurotic and have the weirdest OCD tendencies. Even my family refer to me as 'The weird one' and any friends have a habit of rolling their eyes whenever I speak. However, I'm not mad and this is an opportunity that has been sent by God.

I feel the tears forming in my eyes as I nod slowly. Somehow, I manage to squeak out, "I would love to wait for you, Luke. I'm like you. My job sounds glamorous but most of the time it's mundane. The crew changes along with the destination but the endless routine doesn't. Trips like this are extremely few and far between and just fuel our interest for the run of nights ahead to the holiday destinations of the masses. When I return home at the end of the day, it's to an empty flat that resembles the state of my heart. It's not living, Luke. This is a job for the unattached. The University of my youth that I appear unable to graduate from. Like you, I want more. My sister is also married and has two beautiful children. The worst part is, she is younger than me and I have to pretend most of the time that I wouldn't want my life any other way. But I do. This bubble we live in is gradually running out of air. It once excited me but now I crave the ordinary. This is no longer my dream, Luke. I want much more."

Luke smiles, and a look passes between us. Two lost souls finding a common bond. Both wanting the same things and hoping against hope that the answer is looking right back at them. Maybe this could work. Maybe my fears were unfounded. Maybe everything will work out and I will live happily ever after. Yes, this is fate, I knew it as soon as I laid eyes on Luke. Something ignited inside me and it wasn't just lust. It was a meeting of hearts and somehow my Angel cat Blackie has worked a miracle. In wrecking one marriage forever, he has given me my future. And what a future it is.

~*~*~*~*~

Chapter 33

I think I must glide back to the Emporio on a cloud of love. Luke's hand is firmly in mine and any doubts I ever had are left behind at that amazing little town in the mountains.

As we enter the hotel, the first person I see is Elvis and I realise that in all my happiness, I completely forgot about Marcus.

Feeling the anxiety rushing back, I drag Luke over to the little desk that Elvis calls home. He smiles as he sees us coming and I feel hopeful that Marcus has been found.

"Hello Becca, Luke." He smiles happily, and I breathe a sigh of relief.

"Hey, Elvis. Has Marcus returned?"

He nods happily.

"Yes, he came to see me after breakfast. He was fine and just stayed with his friend for the night. He is outside by the pool if you want to find him."

Smiling at Elvis, I drag Luke behind me purposefully. Marcus better have a good reason for going MIA and I can't wait to hear all the juicy details.

We find him lying next to Rachel, who I notice has Mark on her other side. My heart sinks once again and I look at Luke with worry. He shakes his head and whispers. "Don't jump to conclusions. I'm sure they are just friends. Mark knows she is married."

Shaking my head, I wonder if Luke is slightly mad. I can see very plainly that they are most certainly not and probably never have been - friends! I know this for a fact because I know my friend. She is wearing her sexiest bikini and I see the way her eyes sparkle as she laughs at something he says. They are facing each other and if looks could rival the intensity of the sun, the one he is shooting her would win. I just hope that the only thing on their menu is a mild dose of flirting because one things for sure, Lorenzo is as far away from Rachel's thoughts as he is physically. This is not good.

We move over and I stand at the foot of Marcus's sunbed and clear my throat. He groans.

"You're in my sun and I need it to recharge my energy."

Rachel looks up and grins.

"Hi, guys. Did you have a good day?"

I shake my head and say harshly. "Never mind about that. What about you, Marcus? Did you not think to tell someone you were having a sleepover? The police were informed, and you were officially a missing person. We thought you may have been raped or murdered or had been shipped off as someone's sex slave."

His face lights up. "Ooh, if only."

I look at him with a hard expression.

"Come on, I want to hear your explanation."

He rolls his eyes and grins.

"You sound just like my mother. Anyway, it was nothing. As you know I was in Los Romanticos with Elvis. We were on a high after the officer's party and not ready to call it a night. Well, you would never believe it but a face that I recognised came into the club in the early hours."

I sit down on his sunbed and look interested.

"Who was it? Do I know him?"

Shaking his head, Marcus looks wistful.

"Not unless you are a paid-up member of the Purple Coconut."

I look at Luke in confusion as Rachel giggles. Shaking my head, I say, "What's the Purple Coconut when it's at home?"

Marcus laughs. "It's a gay club in Brighton. One of the best and membership is hard to get hold of. Well, B.A. Bobby is one of its regulars and one of the craziest guys around. Everyone wants to be his friend and more because this guy is seriously hot."

I share a look with Rachel and she giggles. "B.A. Bobby is short for British Airways Bobby. He works for the national airline - apparently and is something of a legend."

Marcus smiles dreamily.

"I couldn't believe my luck when he recognised me. Ooh, I've wanted a piece of that action for as long as I can remember. Well, all my dreams came true because he zeroed in on me like a Hawk on a mouse, and latched himself onto me ready to blow my world."

Luke nudges me as I try to shake the image of B.A. Bobby blowing Marcus's world.

He leans back on his sunbed with a smug look.

"So, you see, I wasn't going to leave the best thing that has ever happened to me just to tell you all where I was. Bobby wasn't here for long, just minimum rest, you know what British Airways are like. Unlike Jet Air they squeeze every working hour from their crew due to their impressive route options. So, there you have it. I found my dream in Acapulco and my life will never be the same again."

I smile at him, glad that he too has found happiness. Wow, Acapulco is like Cupid's home. He must be staying here too because the number of arrows he's flinging about makes me think he has a holiday home here.

I look at Marcus with excitement.

"So, are you seeing him when you return?"

Shaking his head, he looks a little wistful.

"I'm not sure. The trouble is, B.A. Bobby is something of a celebrity in Brighton and Hove and all surrounding areas. He won't be tied down and needs to be free to flit around like a butterfly. I may see him from time to time in the Purple Coconut but I'm realistic. This was my moment and I may never get another one. I expect it will just be a memory to share with my jealous friends when I return. And what a memory it is."

He sighs, and I feel a little unsettled. Despite everything, we have all lived the dream this week. Marcus is the most realistic of us all though. He knows that you wake up from dreams and is fine with it. Jo will be fine, she has her 'happy ever after' assured. Jenny, Rachel and I do not. We have a testing time ahead of us and when the plane lands at Gatwick, everything may change.

~*~*~*~*~

Chapter 34

Luke and I grab a couple of sunbeds and take in the last session of sunbathing of the trip. I am going to miss this. We just don't have the same heat in the UK. The sun has shed most of its power when it heads our way and we always get the dregs of it. Most of the time it misses us altogether and I wonder what it must be like to live in a country where sunshine on the daily menu is a given.

In the UK cloud and rain is a given. The green fields of home may be grateful for it but I would trade it for sunshine every time.

It isn't long before Jenny and Flynn join us. I notice that Jenny is carrying some large shopping bags and look at her with curiosity.

"Did you find the Mall, Jenny? I didn't know there was one here otherwise I would have been there like a bullet from a gun."

Jenny grins. "I bought us all a little something for tonight."

Rachel looks at me and we look at Jenny with interest. She laughs with excitement.

"Well, as it's our last night, I thought we should do something special. After all, this trip has changed my life forever, and I wanted to mark the occasion."

We watch her rummage around in one of the bags and she removes what appears to be an item of clothing from the bag with a flourish.

"Tada!"

Rachel looks at me with a stunned expression and I hear Luke snort beside me. Jenny looks at us with excitement. "So, what do you think? I thought we could all wear them out on the town. It will be fun."

Rachel looks at me with horror and I stifle a giggle. Jenny is holding the most outrageous monstrosity of a dress that I have ever seen. It is made up of frills like a mini flamenco dancer's dress. The material is green and covered in every tropical bird out there. Parrots, flamingos, and puffins. They all adorn the hideous creation and I think I am speechless. Jenny takes our silence as excitement and grins.

"I couldn't resist them. My mum loved her birds, and it was as if it were a sign. There were only four dresses left, and it was buy one get one free. She would love the thought of us all wearing them on our final night and it will be a great memory to take home with us."

Marcus looks up and laughs loudly.

"You maniac, Jenny. Those dresses are hilarious. When you've finished with them can I have one? I would be the envy of everyone in my local if I rocked up in one of those for Salsa night."

Jenny grins and I try to wipe the horror from my face. This is a nightmare. There is no way on God's earth that I want to be seen dead in one of those dresses but how can I refuse? It would be like kicking a wounded puppy. Jenny is recovering well but I know she is still on edge. So, I just smile at her and nod, trying to muster up some enthusiasm.

"Sure, it will be fun."

I try not to look at Luke and Mark who I sense are grinning at each other. Rachel shares my tortured looks but disguises it with a smile.

"Of course, your mum would love it. It's a fitting tribute."

Jenny flings us a bag each and turns to Flynn.

"Come on, let's go and deliver Jo hers and then we can go and get ready."

I look at her in surprise.

"We've got hours before dinner, why the rush?"

Flynn grins as Jenny giggles.

"Let's just say, Flynn and I take a long time to get ready. We may ... um ... be in our room for quite some time."

Rachel grins at me as I laugh softly.

"Of course, see you later guys. Oh, and thanks, Jenny. It's a lovely idea."

I watch them head off hand in hand and my heart melts. Good for Jenny. If one thing has come out of this trip, it's the sight of her happiness. Mission accomplished.

"This is a bloody nightmare."

I stifle a giggle as Rachel grins at me. Jo is furious. She looks ridiculous in her frilly creation and it's only the sight of her that keeps me from crying. These dresses are hideous.

Rachel shakes her head. "We look like some sort of girl band from the seventies. Jenny seems happy though."

We look over and see her flamenco dancing in front of Flynn, who is clapping wildly. She is laughing and looks so happy my heart melts.

"It's only one night. We can put up with looking like this if it makes her happy. If she leaves then we must make the most of having her in our lives."

Jo nods, looking a little ashamed. "You're right. It's only one night and I'm sure after a few tequilas it won't seem so bad."

Pete comes over and I watch her eyes light up. Ever since their reconciliation we have hardly seen the two of them. They have been seconded in their room for most of the time we had left. I'm glad to see they are back on track because they make the sweetest couple in the world. Jo can be abrupt and hard sometimes but she has a soft heart. We started at Jet Air together and a better friend I couldn't have wished to find. You know where you are with Jo. She doesn't pull any punches and tells it how it is. However, she is kind and generous and isn't one to gossip. I trust her completely and know that she deserves her happy ever after with Pete. At first, I was sceptical when they got together. Pete was a hot new captain that was an instant hit with the crew. He is fun and good company and there were many girls, and guys I might add, that were after him. However, he only ever had eyes for Jo. They clicked on a stopover one night and have been inseparable ever since. It wasn't long before she moved in with him and in pure Jo practical fashion, rented her flat out instead. This latest drama was out of character for them both and I hope that it's smooth sailing from here on in.

There are a lot of us tonight, so we are meeting in the bar. Our numbers have grown considerably over the length of this trip and my heart sinks as I spy Mark cosying up to Rachel. Oh well, only one more night of worry and then she will return to face her future. Vowing to keep a close eye on my friend, I head over to join them.

Luke is grabbing us some drinks and I sit down next to Rachel and roll my eyes.

"Well, this is different."

Rachel laughs.

"I never thought I'd wear a dress like this in my life. There must be strictly no photographic evidence of it because I would never live it down."

Laughing, I gesture towards Marcus who is snapping away on his phone.

"Too late, Marcus has already downloaded it to Facebook."

Rachel looks annoyed.

"Typical Marcus. Nothing is sacred."

Jenny dances over, pulling a smiling Flynn behind her.

"Hey, guys. Thanks for wearing the dresses. They're amazing, aren't they?"

I laugh softly. "You could say that."

They squash in beside us as Luke returns with a bottle of tequila and some shot glasses.

He grins. "One for the road?"

Like giggling teenagers, we line up the shots and then raise our glasses simultaneously. Luke says loudly.

"To Mexico and the best damn honeymoon, a guy could get."

Slamming our glasses down we take the hit and shake our heads as we feel the burn. Coughing, I look at Luke and squeak, "You forgot to add the lemonade."

He laughs. "No, I didn't. Tonight, there are no half measures. This is our last night and we must make it count."

The others cheer as he refills the glasses and I laugh to myself. "Yes, lots of alcohol is needed to mend the hole in my heart at what tomorrow will bring."

We head out to a nearby restaurant and I think the waiter pales considerably when he sees the huge party bearing down on him. Everyone is in high spirits and we draw many a curious look. I don't care though because I have everything I need holding my hand. I laugh as I see Flynn running down the street with Jenny on his back and Jo and Pete holding hands and laughing together.

Once inside we are given a large table made up of several pushed together. The noise is off the scale as we all chatter excitedly. Elvis is laughing at something Marcus is saying and I know he will miss us when we have gone. They are two of a kind and their friendship has been one of the sweetest things to come out of this trip.

Luke puts his arm around me and whispers.

"I know you hate that dress but there is something incredibly sexy about it."

He runs his fingers down my shoulder and I feel a delicious shiver inside. Way to go Becca. Bullseye, hole in one and Olympic gold. I feel as if I have won the jackpot in the love lottery with Luke. I want nothing more than to be alone with him for the time we have left. He appears unable to keep his hands off me even for a second and I absolutely love it.

We listen to Jo talking about the wedding - again. She chatters on as Pete just nods and smiles at her indulgently. She looks at us and smiles.

"We're going to have so much fun planning this wedding together. I'll arrange a planning session as soon as possible. I actually can't wait to get started. There is so much to do, and I will need one of those bride planning books that they sell in W H Smith. I've always wanted one and now I can, it's a dream come true."

She claps her hands. "This is going to be the best wedding in history."

Rachel smiles but I see the sadness in her eyes.

I whisper, "Are you ok?"

She nods sadly.

"I was as excited as Jo once. My wedding was the best day of my life. Everything was perfect, and I had the rest of my life to enjoy my new husband. It certainly is a dream come true and I just hope that Jo doesn't wake up from her dream as quickly as I have."

I worry at her words. It's as if she has given up on Lorenzo already. I smile reassuringly.

"It's just an argument. You'll get through it. It's what tests marriages. You'll see, Lorenzo will have missed you and you him. It's my bet that as soon as you set eyes on him again you will wonder why you had doubts. Just you wait and see."

She smiles thinly, and I can tell she doesn't believe a word I've said. As she turns to Mark, I see the spark ignite in her eyes again and sigh inside. Despite my optimism, I can tell that Rachel has given up on her marriage already. I will just have to be there for her when her world comes crashing down around her.

~*~*~*~*~

Chapter 35

So, here it is, the moment of truth. We are all packed and ready after a fashion. That rug/blanket thing of Captain Elviras refuses to be contained in my suitcase. Instead, I have just rolled it up in true Ali Baba fashion and tied it with a piece of string that Elvis found for me.

Luke is also packed, and we stare at each other with stricken expressions. If it's any consolation, Luke looks as upset as I feel, and he sighs heavily.

"So, the honeymoon is over and now back to reality."

I nod miserably. "Yes, life will seem extremely dull after the excitement of this week."

I watch as he moves across and offers me his hand.

Come on, let's go and take one last look at the view; I don't want to forget a thing."

I follow him to the balcony and my heart wrenches as I see the beautiful sparkling sea that surrounds the bay. Luke puts his arm around my shoulders and draws me close.

"I'm going to miss this - us, Becca."

I nod sadly. "Me too. It's been like a dream for the best part of a week. Despite what you may think, trips just aren't usually like this."

Luke laughs softly. "I'm glad to hear it."

Then he turns to face me and pulls me close, tilting my face to his and whispers.

"I'm going to miss this place, but most of all I'm going to miss you."

He lowers his lips to mine and I feel my heart breaking inside. How can I bear this, it feels so final? Despite our best intentions things will never be the same again. Real life has a habit of intruding and it will probably fizzle out. Luke will return to patrolling the nautical Neverland and I will return to the mundane drinks service. My days off will be spent organising a cupboard in my flat and striving for excellence in the housework department. Worst of all is the thought of my empty flat waiting for me. There is no one to talk to and no life outside of work to speak of.

Luke pulls back and looks at me sadly.

"Come on, let's get this over with."

With a sigh, I follow him inside and take one last look at the Love Palace. I laugh softly. "I'm going to miss this room. Despite everything, I've got used to it now. It almost feels like home and it will seem strange that my bed doesn't move beneath me when I tuck myself in later on tonight."

I look at him sadly. "It will also feel strange to be alone again."

My lip trembles as the realisation hits home. Alone again! As always and 100% certain. Despite all our best intentions I'm a realist and know that real life will get in the way. This is it, the best week of my life has ended and the only thing I really have left are my memories.

Luke looks at me with concern and pulls me tightly against him. I hear his heart beating loudly within that strong, hard chest of lustness.

He growls. "This is our beginning, Becca. This is where it began but is most certainly not where it ends. We will find a way, I will make sure of it."

Then he kisses me so passionately my toes curl. All thoughts leave me but one. I will cling onto this man with everything I have. If I have to enlist in the Navy, I will because some things are worth fighting for. I'm not talking about my country here - oh no, I will fight for my man because now I have found him, I am never letting him go.

The flight home is in direct contrast to the one out here. There is no excitement, and everyone is feeling depressed and quiet. Luke is no longer the man in 12A. He has been upgraded to First Class sexy man. He is now sitting in luxury being totally spoiled by Rachel. Jo is no longer angry and is fussing over Pete by taking him in lots of drinks and food, arranged with little love messages on the side. Jenny is quiet and has withdrawn back into herself. I understand why though. At least I still have Luke for a few more hours, but watching Jenny and Flynn's goodbye was heart-breaking. Like me, she must have doubts and I hope that she doesn't lose the freedom of the person she has become.

Rachel is quiet and preoccupied, and I wonder what really happened with her and Mark. More than most she must be dreading returning home. At least my drama will end at the cabin door on arrival. Hers will be just beginning.

Marcus nudges me back to the here and now.

"Cheer up, Becca. There's always another trip."

I smile shakily. "Yes, not like this one though."

He nods thoughtfully. "Yes, it was certainly eventful. I must say I had the time of my life. I told Elvis I would try to get on another trip soon. He told me that next time he would take a few days off and take me to his hometown and show me a wild time. Apparently, they make Brighton sound like retirement city with the stories he tells. I'm going to make it my mission to chat up Tristan in crewing. It's imperative I get out here, pronto."

I smile. "Then get one for Jenny too. She will be hounding him too if I know her."

Marcus grins. "Yes, this trip has been surprising in a lot of ways. Jenny's transformation was astonishing. I hope it continues and doesn't fizzle out when we return to the familiar."

As I follow him out into the cabin with my drinks cart, I pray that we all get our happy ever after. I wonder where we will be this time next year.

~*~*~*~*~

Chapter 36

One Year Later

As I stare out of the window, it all comes rushing back to me. One year already. This time last year my world ended.

I remember the pain I felt when I watched Luke walk away. He left me in the same position as the one where I saw him for the first time. As goodbyes went, it was quick and clinical. There was no time for tears and no long drawn out emotional goodbyes. The fact he was seated in First-Class meant he got to leave first. As it turned out, he couldn't get off there quickly enough.

Sighing, I turn away from the window and remember how my heart broke in two. I returned home to my empty flat and even the sight of Malcolm with his new flower did nothing to lift my spirits. Luke was gone and once again I was alone.

I still remember what happened as if it were yesterday.

I had taken a break and went to sit with Luke in the First-Class cabin. He had been pre-occupied most of the flight with catching up on emails and communications on his iPad. I still remember the look he gave me when he told me that he had to return to the submarine. All leave was cancelled, and they were being recalled as a matter of urgency. They were needed due to a diplomatic incident, and the mission was top secret.

I still remember the pain in my heart as he spoke. I tried to push away the doubts. This all seemed too convenient, too unbelievable and very much an escape plan. The Sailorettes words played on repeat in my brain as

I tried to stay strong and pretend I understood. But I didn't. I wasn't strong, and it took all my inner strength not to shatter into a million pieces around him. There was to be no meeting of the parents and no extended honeymoon period. This was reality biting, and it bit hard.

Luke appeared upset, but I could tell I had lost him already. His mind was suddenly back in the game and he seemed on edge and anxious.

I bite my lip as I remember the pain I felt when he walked away from me. Would I ever see him again? A small part of me had hope. However, the larger more practical part that I hate was admonishing me severely for ever thinking a man like Luke would want a woman like me.

My thoughts are interrupted by a knock on the door.

Shaking away the unpleasant memories, I move across and open it. Loud shrieks fill my ears as Jenny bowls into the room like a whirlwind.

"Becca, oh my God, I can't believe it's today. Who would have thought it would be today of all days? I actually can't contain my excitement."

I grin. "No, neither can I. Have you seen Jo this morning?"

She laughs softly. "In full Bridezilla mode. I heard her ticking off one of the receptionists about the noise outside her room last night. Apparently, she didn't sleep a wink due to the lift moving endlessly up and down all night. She was moaning that she would have huge dark circles under her eyes and look older than her years. She also said she wouldn't blame Pete if he took one look at her walking down that aisle and ran for the hills."

I grin and smile at Jenny softly.

"You seem so happy Jenny. A traveller's life agrees with you."

She laughs happily and runs and jumps onto the bed. She stretches out and groans.

"Ooh, this bed is so soft. It's been a hard few months on the ranch. I forgot how luxurious a double bed is."

I laugh as I see her splayed out enjoying the comfort.

Moving across I join her and lie beside her contemplating the ceiling.

"Do you have any regrets, Jenny?"

She laughs softly.

"None at all. Leaving Jet Air was the best decision I ever made. I couldn't get back to Flynn fast enough and even though I managed to get on another trip to see him, the month dragged by interminably."

I smile at her happiness. Jenny did indeed leave everything behind and follow Flynn to Mexico. They didn't stay there long though. They were soon on the move and travelled extensively throughout the year. They have just finished a stint on a Ranch in Arizona where they lived as cowboys for two months, earning their bed and board by working on the land. Jenny has never been happier, you can tell. Her shy ways disappeared under the bright lights of that hypnotist's stage and never returned. She became Amazonian Jenny and has never looked back. One year on and she is still madly in love with her crazy surfer dude and living the dream. She rents out her mother's home and stumbles from one crazy adventure to another. Life is good for Jenny and Flynn and even though we see so little of her, I wouldn't want it any other way.

Jenny interrupts my thoughts.

"Well, this is all very nice and all, but I have been sent here on a mission that cannot be ignored."

I laugh softly. "And that is?"

She grins. "Instructions from our leader. We must meet for breakfast in the matrimonial suite. There's no getting out of it I'm afraid, you are to attend whether you like it or not."

Grinning, I look down at my large fluffy white dressing gown and raise my eyes.

"Can't I even get dressed first?"

Jenny giggles. "No, come as you are. It won't matter it's only us after all."

As she pulls me from the bed I feel the excitement stirring within me. Today is going to be a good day.

We take the short walk down the carpeted hallway to Jo's suite of rooms. The hotel is silent, and I wonder what secrets the doors we pass contain.

As we reach the huge oak doors of the Presidential Suite, I feel the excitement grip me. I can't wait to get started.

We knock loudly on the door and almost instantly it opens, and I grin as I see Rachel smiling happily at us.

"Come in, Princess Bridey is holding court this morning and you're late."

We laugh and follow her inside.

The Presidential suite is amazing. It's made up of several rooms all leading off the beautiful sitting room we find ourselves in. There is a little seating area set around a huge window overlooking the grounds. I can see the breakfast has arrived and my stomach growls as I smell the delights waiting for us.

We take our seats and wait for the bride herself to join us.

I look at Rachel and my heart leaps as I see the happiness in her eyes. It's been a tough year for her, but she appears to have come out of it intact and happy.

As she offers me some bucks fizz, I smile.

"How are things, Rachel? Is everything sorted now?"

She shakes her head. "Nearly. I'm just waiting for the decree absolute and then I will no longer be Rachel Marcini. I will be plain old Rachel Mitchell again and happier for it."

She takes a sip of her drink and laughs. "Maybe today isn't the best day to celebrate a conscious uncoupling."

We all laugh, and I think back to what happened when Rachel returned home.

It appears that she wasn't the only one having lustful thoughts in the week she was away. Lorenzo, it seems had been enjoying himself while the cat was away, and she found him in a compromising position inside the food cupboard at the restaurant. It turned out that he had been sleeping with one of the waitresses in her absence and had decided that she was much more suitable wife material than his own.

I laugh as I remember that Rachel had apparently thrown every packet in the cupboard at them while screaming blue murder. By the time they exited the cupboard they looked like they had done ten rounds in a food fight boxing ring. The arguments that followed were intense and soul destroying, and it wasn't an easy time for them both. I should know because I gained a flatmate and had to listen to every detail of their marriage breakdown as it happened. Seeing Rachel today looking happy and animated makes my heart swell. It was a dark time, and I worried about her. She sank into a depression brought on by the thought that she had failed at her marriage. I think every emotion going passed through her this last year and it was a difficult time. Life has a habit of working things out though and I smile at her happily.

"Did Mark arrive safely?"

I smile as I see the spark ignite in her eyes as they sparkle with excitement.

"Yes, I picked him up from the airport last night. He's off for three weeks and we are heading off on holiday to Antigua after the wedding. I can't wait as this last few months have been hell."

Jenny looks at her with interest.

"What happened again? I forgot how you both got back in touch."

Rachel smiles.

"Well, as you know nothing happened in Acapulco, despite being extremely tempted. We kept in touch though and shared the odd Skype call and email. He helped me through a tough time and was just there for me whenever I needed someone to vent off to."

She looks at me and smiles softly.

"Although Becca did an amazing job of that herself. You know, I will always be grateful for you getting me through it, don't you babe?"

I nod and a look passes between us. The look of a true friendship that has shared the worst and best of times. Rachel and I are like sisters. We have a bond that will never be broken because of what we have shared during the worst moments of our lives. We got through an incredibly tough year with our friendship to hold us close and comfort our battered souls.

I was so happy when Rachel's friendship with Mark took off. She met him on his next trip home and they took up where they left off in Acapulco. Contrary to reports, Mark wasn't the philandering sailor that he was painted as, and they are the sweetest couple in the world. I should know because they stayed in my flat for a whole week on his last trip home. I got to know him quite well and discovered that he is perfect for Rachel in every way. I am happy that it worked out for them.

As I take a sip of my bubble filled drink, I hear the unmistakable tones of my friend approaching.

"For goodness sake, mother, this is a disaster. Find Crispin and sort it out with him. It's what he's paid for and I can't deal with this now. You will just have to sort it out with him instead."

I look at my three friends and grin. Here we go.

~*~*~*~*~

Chapter 37

Jo rushes into the room and rolls her eyes. "Mothers, huh?"

I sneak a look at Jenny and feel a pang as I see the desolation in her eyes. Reaching out, I take her hand and smile. "Not all of them, hey Jenny. I would imagine your mum would be happiness personified on your wedding day."

I feel bad as I see the tears form in her eyes and she smiles bravely.

"Yes, my mum would have been amazing. She would have loved Flynn and I wish more than anything she could have met him. They would have got on so well."

Rachel smiles softly.

"She's watching, Jenny. On every trip you take and every corner you turn she is with you. Your memories keep her alive and your heart holds her dear. She may not be with you physically but will always be a part of you. When you look in the mirror, her eyes stare back at you. You are a part of her that lives and breathes, and she will be so proud of what you've become."

I think the tears fall down everyone's faces as we take in Rachel's words. Jenny looks around and laughs softly.

"Well, I hope she doesn't see everything, Rachel. I'm not sure I can bear the thought of her watching Flynn and me, you know ... um ... oh well, you get my drift."

We all laugh, and Rachel says loudly.

"I know what you mean. If there is an afterlife, I will certainly have some explaining to do to any passed relatives watching over me. I'm just praying they are discreet up there."

Jenny laughs and I'm glad that the mood has lightened. This day is going to be emotional enough as it is.

Once breakfast is out of the way, we all head back to our respective rooms to get ready for the wedding. There is much to do what with hair, makeup and all the pampering that goes with staging such a show. As I make my way back to my room, I think about how far we've all come in a year. When Luke walked away from me he took my heart with him. I'm not sure how I functioned for the next few weeks after he left. It was business as usual in the hard light of day. It would have been better not to have met him than live with the loss. But I did and somehow, I got by.

Once again, my thoughts are interrupted as a door opens nearby and I see Marcus racing out dressed in all his usher finery. I laugh softly as his hands fly up to his face and he exclaims,

"Good God, Becca. You gave me a fright, and it's not just because of what you're wearing. I mean, Terry Towelling is so last season, darling."

We exchange the grin of the familiar and I feel myself relaxing. Marcus always has that effect on me although I have no idea why. I mean, he's so highly strung he could win Wimbledon.

He looks me up and down. "Hm, Crispin would have fifty fits if he saw you now. You really should be in hair and makeup, my dear."

I laugh softly.

"Well, you certainly started early, Marcus. You've scrubbed up very well if you don't mind me saying."

He rolls his eyes and giggles. "Oh, this old thing. I've had it for years."

I laugh as his suit is definitely not one anyone would want to hold onto for too long. He is dressed head to toe in a powder blue suit with cream braiding. His shirt is pale pink and ruffles adorn the front of it. I should have known he had a penchant for these after his desire for the hideous flamenco dress. He has a large pink gerbera in his buttonhole and his hair is slicked back. All in all, he looks like a crooner from the 50s.

I smile, biting back the raucous laughter that I'm holding at bay at the sight before me. As if he senses it he rolls his eyes. "The things we do for love."

I nod, my lips twitching at the sight before me. I look at him with interest.

"So, what's the plan?"

He looks around furtively and moves closer. Leaning towards me, he whispers,

"You know that it's the law that the bridesmaid gets off with the best man at these things?"

I raise my eyes, "Not in this case."

He grins. "As I thought. So, I am offering my services to prevent bad luck descending and ruining the day. Tonight, darling, I am re-writing history and it is the usher getting it on with the extremely delectable wedding planner."

We burst out laughing and I shake my head.

"You're out of control, Marcus."

He grins. "It's all your fault, honey. If you hadn't insisted I accompany you all to every dress fitting and wedding shenanigan going, I would never have fallen crazily in lust with the man holding it all together. He won't know what's hit him when I unleash the beast on him later tonight."

He winks, and I shake my head to erase the picture I now have of Marcus's beast.

He looks at his watch and screams.

"Oh, my giddy Aunt, we only have three hours before showtime. Get going my darling and transform into a thing of great beauty. I need to go and offer my services to our glorious leader."

He rushes off waving his hands in the air and I smile.

How I love him. He has been the best friend a girl could get this last year. We have become almost inseparable as I accompanied him to every gay bar in Brighton. He was just what I needed to heal a devastated heart and I will love him forever.

It wasn't just me but Rachel too. We were a solid threesome for much of the year and the most dysfunctional trio you could ever wish to meet. I wonder if Crispin Dupont knows what's heading his way?

As I enter my room, I laugh at the thought of our glorious wedding planner. Crispin Dupont, founder and manager of Dream days, the ultimate in wedding planning services. Jo was determined to sign him up and I can see why. Although he doesn't come cheap, he has been a godsend. He has powered through the preparations leaving no stone left unturned. He has organised every flower and table present. He planned the venue, the seating plan, the menu, and the flowers. Every little touch has been his creation, and he has come up with ideas that have never been thought of before. All in all, Crispin was worth every last pound that he charged.

Once again, I wander over to the window and watch the hustle and bustle below. My room overlooks the garden and I watch the workers equip the Marquee that has been set up in the grounds of this amazing stately home just for the occasion.

As I lean against the window frame, my mind wanders once more.

Luke and I kept in touch although our communication was few and far between. He was occupied in diverting a national incident and communications were limited. It wasn't the same sharing the odd text or Skype call. Whenever I saw him virtually, he looked tired and strained. The magic disappeared, and real life had taken over. We were trapped in a strange situation. We were apart before we had ever really been together. The only memory we had to talk about was Mexico and soon the conversation dried up. We tried to keep the interest going, but it was hard over the Internet to recapture the euphoria that only a close relationship can bring.

A loud knock at the door interrupts my thoughts and I feel a flutter of excitement. Here we go. Showtime.

~*~*~*~

Chapter 38

"I can't believe this is really happening."

I look at Jo and words fail me. She looks stunning. Rachel sighs and I watch the tears form in her eyes. "You all look gorgeous."

I smile at her happily. "So do you. You've always suited blue, it brings out the colour of your eyes."

Rachel blushes and Jenny laughs. "Now your pink cheeks match my dress."

Laughing, I look over at Jenny who looks amazing in the pale pink creation that hugs her curves like a second skin.

Jo's eyes mist over, and she says quietly.

"I think we all look amazing. I can't believe it's really happening though. I mean, only one year ago today I couldn't stand Pete. I would have thought you were mad if you told me where I would be in a years' time. The way I was feeling I would have thrown myself off of that cliff with the divers we never got to see."

Jenny laughs. "Poor Pete. Did you ever find out who Margaret was?"

Jo grins. "No, we didn't. Although I know who she is now."

Rachel giggles. "Where is the little terror?"

"With our neighbour, Mrs Mathewson. She couldn't come today because she has visitors, so she offered to babysit."

Jenny smiles sadly. "I always wanted a little puppy. There's no way that will happen with all the travelling we do. Maybe one day when we settle down."

Jo snorts. "I'd like to see that day. You're both having way too much fun to think about settling down in one place."

I look at Jenny with interest. "If you did where would it be?"

She shrugs. "Possibly Australia. Flynn's family are there, and it was always expected that he would take over his father's company one day. He is just sowing his wild oats, as his father calls it, before he has to take his rightful position."

We all look surprised and Rachel says what we're all dying to know.

"What business is it?"

Jenny looks annoyed. "Oh, some boring corporation that employs about a million people worldwide. It's no wonder Flynn got out when he could."

Jo looks as stunned as I feel. "Goodness me, Jenny. Are you saying that Flynn's family are wealthy?"

She shrugs. "You could say that. I think they have a home in every country that they have a business. His father has a Private Jet that he uses to keep track of them all and they own half of Sydney. Flynn hates it all though and wants the simple life. The trouble is, he's an only child so will have to head back some time or another. We're thinking of heading back at Christmas to say hi."

Rachel looks at me and bursts out laughing. "Only you could land a billionaire, Jenny. The funniest thing about it is you don't give a damn."

Jenny shakes her head.

"I'm just happy when it's just Flynn and me. This last year has been the best of my life because I've got to spend it with him. We're not into material possessions and just want to experience everything while we still can."

She looks excited. "After the wedding, we are going to Africa to help build an Orphanage. I can't wait because apparently, we will have to live in tents and eat army rations. I've always wanted to go to Africa and now's my chance."

Jo shakes her head in bewilderment.

"I'll never understand you, Jenny. Flynn could pay for you to see the world in five-star luxury and you just want to backpack your way around it. I always thought it but now I know you're mad."

We all grin at her and Jenny smiles. "Like I said, I only want Flynn. I have a feeling that the money would just complicate things. When we do head back there, the business would take him away from me and that isn't worth any amount of money. At the moment he's all mine and mine alone. This is the most special time of my life and I intend on guarding it for as long as possible."

My eyes fill up and I move across and hug her tightly.

"You're right, honey. You take every moment you can get and hold onto it and never let it go. What you and Flynn have is precious, and no amount of money could buy it. Good for you, you do things your own way or not at all."

As I stand hugging Jenny, the others join us. We all stand huddled together - well as close as we can get given that we're all dressed in meringues.

Jo says in an emotional voice.

"Promise that we will never change. We will always be friends and here for each other through thick and thin."

We all nod with a firm resolve and echo her words. "Through thick and thin."

"Ladies, ladies, I can't leave you alone for five minutes. Just look at the mess you're making of those fantastic creations."

We pull back as Crispin clicks his fingers and his team rushes forth to smooth us down and repair our makeup. Jo looks across at me and smiles brightly. It's time.

Twenty minutes later we are standing outside the room where the wedding is taking place. We stand nervously waiting and I feel my heart fluttering wildly. Jo is silent beside me. I hear her taking deep breaths as she tries to contain the emotion that threatens to ruin the immaculate makeup that has transformed her into a blushing bride. Jenny smiles at me and I think how pretty she looks. Love has certainly agreed with her and her eyes sparkle as she gazes at me with excitement. "Are you ok, Becca?"

I swallow hard and smile nervously. "I think so."

Jo and Rachel smile at us and I think how lucky I am. If I had one good friend, I would count myself lucky. But I have always been greedy and have four who I can't love more than I do.

We hear the music start and Crispin appears looking anxious. He starts to talk softly into his headset and then looks at us with pride.

"Positions everyone. The show's about to start."

I take one look at Jo and we share a smile. She grabs my hand and says softly.

"You look beautiful, Becca."

I grin. "Right back at you."

I watch as she turns to take her father's outstretched arm and I see the pride in his face. It's a beautiful moment and I don't want to miss a thing. Then, as the doors open I turn to my left and see the same look on my father's face as I take his arm. He says huskily, "You look beautiful baby girl."

The tears spring to my eyes as I look at the proud man about to finally give his daughter away. I laugh softly. "About time, hey dad?"

He raises my hand to his lips and kisses it and then clasps it tightly.

"You will always be my baby girl, married or not."

We share the look of one chapter ending and one beginning before I turn to face the man who claimed my heart. As the doors open my eyes look at nothing else but the sight of my future waiting for me at the end of a flower-festooned aisle. Luke, my husband, my soul mate and my incredibly sexy merman. Whoever thought I would be so lucky?

Seeing him standing there watching me, my mind returns to that day. Three months were up, and I was due to meet him from his flight. I was about to leave when there was a knock at the door. I felt irritated because I was running late and didn't want to tarnish his homecoming by making him wait around.

I flung the door open with a frown and my world stopped still.

Filling the doorway was the most fantastic sight in the world. Luke.

The months just fell away as we drank in the sight of each other like someone who had just had their sight restored. Just for a second, we stood - just looking. Then with one step, we were in each other's arms and I hung on for grim death. As Luke kissed me like a man possessed, I kissed him back like a starving woman, deprived for so long. It was as if the doubts and worries faded away and *we knew*. This was real, and we were home.

The happy memories accompany me down the aisle. I notice nobody but him. His gorgeous eyes are trained on me and me alone. He pulls me towards him like a gravitational force and I remember how everything just fell into place.

Luke never returned to sea. He told me that he had just endured the worst three months of his life and had handed in his flippers, or whatever they have to hand back. He took a position at the Head Office in Admiralty house. Far from being a desk job though, he travels around the country doing whatever a landlubber submariner does.

We live in my flat and I am still with Jet Air. This suits us for now. Once we are married, we may tread a different path, but this year has been a whirlwind and I think we need to let life settle down first.

I am conscious of my best friend as she walks to her future alongside me. It was her suggestion to combine our big days.

Luke asked me to marry him exactly one week after he returned. He took me for a romantic meal and hid the ring in the dessert like they do on the films. Luckily for me, I had the wet wipes handy which saved me from an anxiety attack at the thought of slipping a cream encrusted diamond on my clinically clean finger.

I was more than happy to join forces with Jo and Pete because it saved us an absolute fortune and meant that we didn't have to wait too long. I have waited long enough to find Luke. It doesn't matter that we are sharing the best day of our life because we are sharing it with two amazing people who I love.

As I draw near Luke smiles the same smile that sets my soul on fire and makes my toes curl. He nods to my father with the respect he deserves and takes my hand, clasping it tightly like a precious stone that he needs to keep safe. His eyes throw little sparkles of love into mine and I melt inside.

Jo and Pete start the ball rolling and we await our turn patiently. I listen to my friend declare her love for the man who idolises her and then it is our turn.

As Luke and I declare our love and commitment to each other I feel complete. I think I knew from the moment I set eyes on him that we would arrive at this point. Don't ask me how, I just knew. How we got here was unconventional but all that matters is we did.

Then we seal the deal as the registrar utters those immortal words.

"You may now kiss your brides."

~*~*~*~*~

Epilogue

One Year Later

I giggle and try to loosen Luke's grip around me. "We'll be late, and they will *know*."

He grins. "Know what?"

I blush. "You know, that we...um ... you know."

He rolls over and pulls me on top of him, his arms gripping me to him like a vice.

"Who cares if they *know*. We're married after all. It's what married people do."

I kiss him softly and groan. He laughs.

"Was that a groan, Becca? You know, you really should learn to control your groaning ways."

I giggle into his chest as he tightens his grip if that's at all possible.

"I wonder if you can hear my groans on that porno we made. Maybe they just edited out my groaning ways."

Luke laughs. "I'd pay to see that film. I wonder whether it ever made the large screen, or did it go straight to DVD?"

Laughing, I roll my eyes. "Probably just made the internet. It was pretty bad if I remember rightly."

Luke growls huskily.

"All of this talk of pornos is giving me ideas."

Pulling back, I wink at him sexily.

"Hold that thought, handsome. Like I said, we'll be late, and they will *know*."

Luckily, he releases me, and we reluctantly get ready for the party tonight.

As we clean our teeth side by side in front of the 'his and hers' sinks, I catch his eye in the mirror. Grinning, I look around and mumble.

"Impressive, isn't it?"

He answers with the same toothbrush filled mumble.

"You can say that again."

I grin as I finish brushing my teeth and look around me in awe.

"I never thought Jenny would end up in a place like this. If it was me, I would never want to leave."

Luke nods.

"Me too. This bathroom alone is bigger than our flat and there are ten more of them. Do you think she cares though?"

Laughing, I throw him a towel.

"Not one bit. Jenny would be happy in a tent as long as it was with Flynn. They only agreed to move back because of their situation."

Luke follows me back into the huge bedroom that we have been given for the duration of our trip. We are staying with Jenny and Flynn along with the others. She invited us out to stay and even paid for our tickets to Sydney. We are here for two weeks and I'm looking forward to spending quality time with my friends.

By the time we are ready I'm feeling hungry. Tonight, we are eating in. Apparently, Flynn is the 'King of the Barby' and is looking forward to demonstrating his skills.

We are soon ready and head off to find the others.

"Over here, Becca, Luke."

I look over the huge patio area and see Rachel and Mark sitting side by side in a very comfortable looking seat. Grinning, we rush over. I look around me, exclaiming, "This is amazing, isn't it?"

Rachel smiles.

"It certainly is. Who would have thought Jenny would do so well for herself?"

As if on cue, Jenny races out closely followed by Flynn.

I smile as I see the happiness in her face as she clings to Flynn's hand like the newlyweds they are.

As she sits down, Flynn smiles at us.

"Can I get anyone a beer, or anything else that you want come to think of it?"

Luke smiles and jumps up.

"Here, we'll come and give you a hand."

He turns to Mark

"Let's leave the girls to talk."

He kisses me gently on the lips and walks away with the guys. The others laugh as they see my expression. I grin. "What, can't a wife enjoy a kiss from her husband in public now?"

Jenny laughs. "Kiss away. I do all the time. In fact, we are known as the kissing couple around here. Nobody can believe that we still can't keep our hands off each other, despite the fact we have been inseparable for two years now."

I smile, but notice the light in Jenny's eyes suddenly fade a little.

"Are you ok about all of this, Jenny?"

She sighs and tucks her feet underneath her on the couch.

"I will have to be. I suppose we couldn't keep on travelling. Especially now."

She looks down and pats her tummy with contentment."

Rachel smiles happily.

"How long have you got?"

"Three months and they will be here. We call them Tom and Jerry or Mickey and Minnie, depending on what mood we're in."

I smile at her with excitement.

"You beat us all to it. I still can't get my head around the fact it's twins though. That's madness."

Jenny giggles. "Luckily, the news distracted his parents from the disappointment that we got married in Vegas. They were so upset that Flynn didn't have the big family wedding they wanted."

Rachel looks interested.

"Would you have liked that?"

Jenny shakes her head vehemently.

"I couldn't think of anything worse. No, it was perfect the way it was. Just Flynn, me, the Elvis impersonator and his boyfriend. Perfect."

We laugh as Jo heads over with Marcus in tow.

He squeals when he sees us.

"Ladies, ladies, I can't believe this piece of heaven I'm in. Jenny, you may never see the back of me. I will take up childcare and be your Manny."

Jenny giggles. "Stay as long as you like but I thought you were a wedding planner now?"

Marcus looks over at Crispin who is balancing a couple of bright exotic looking cocktails on a silver tray as he wobbles across to us.

"I am, but you know me, I could change direction. It wouldn't be the first time."

Crispin arrives and hands the very gay drink to his boyfriend. As it turned out Marcus got his guy, and they have been inseparable ever since. He gave up flying to become Crispin's partner in more ways than one. They are extremely popular on the wedding scene and are booked solid for the next three years.

Marcus blows him a kiss as Crispin says shrilly.

"Now, I make a mean margarita and my mojitos are to die for. Any takers?"

Jo says eagerly.

"We'll take everything you've got, Crispin. I want to try them all."

Looking ecstatic at the thought of playing cocktail maker, Crispin hurries off. Jo looks around and smiles at Jenny.

"You know what, Jenny, your mum would be so proud of you. She would never believe what an amazing girl you turned out to be."

Jenny smiles sadly.

"I wish she could be here to share all of this with me. She would have loved to be a grandmother and will miss out on so much, as will we."

Leaning over we all reach for her hands. Rachel says softly.

"Remember she is in your heart, Jenny. Your memories will keep her alive and you will share them with Bart and Lisa when they arrive."

Jo giggles. "I think of them as Pinky and Perky."

Marcus grins. "My favourite is Tinky-Winky and Gaga."

I snort. "Don't you mean, Lala?"

He grins. "No, I mean what I say."

Rolling my eyes, I turn to her.

"Have you thought of names for them?"

Jenny smiles. "Well, if one is a girl then Jacqueline after my mum. If a boy, then Tom after my Dad."

Jo looks interested.

"What if you have two girls or two boys?"

Jenny grins. "Well, that's obvious isn't it?"

We look confused as she laughs.

"It would have to be Elvis for a boy and Margaret for a girl. I had thought of Ernesto, but Flynn overruled me."

Jo looks horrified. "Good God, Jenny, have you gone mad? Why on earth would you inflict such awful names on two sweet little babies?"

Jenny giggles. "As if we would. Gosh, you should have seen your face. No, we haven't decided past those names. We will wait until they arrive before we make any firm decisions."

We are interrupted as the men head back and I smile at Luke as he sits beside me and pulls me close. As he kisses the top of my head I snuggle in beside him and look around at the people I call my *Framily*. Friends and family combined, they are special in so many ways. I actually think we now have it all. Who would have thought that one week away would have changed so many lives forever? What happened in Mexico certainly didn't stay in Mexico and nobody is happier about that than me.

The End

Don't forget to claim your Free Book!

sjcrabb.com

Have You read?

sjcrabb.com

Printed in Great Britain
by Amazon